THE INTIMACY OF LOSS

A Novella

POORNIMA MANCO

Dearest Caroline,

Lots of Love,

Poornima

xx

For my girls
Mahika and Prianka

In the messy business of life, let hope be your
guiding light

CONTENTS

I	1
II	21
III	41
IV	55
V	72
Afterword	87
Acknowledgments	89
About the Author	91
Also by Poornima Manco	93

I

1985

I was fifteen when I first saw her. She had a broom in one hand and was sweeping the street with great gusto. A street sweeper with style, I observed to myself as I shifted my satchel from one shoulder to the other. Upon getting closer to her, I noticed how odd her eyes were. One was brown and the other grey. Her hair had been pulled back into a messy bun, and several bangles jangled on her wrists. Her *salwar kameez* [1]had seen better days, the pattern and colour having faded into a murky grey.

I walked by the side of the road, but in the years since this particular part of the colony had been conceived, the roads had been widened to accommodate the increasing traffic, and now the distance between the front gates of the houses that flanked the road, and the road itself, had shrunk considerably. In addition to that were the trees planted at twenty-feet intervals, which made walking as interesting as an obstacle course. You'd walk for a bit on the dusty sidewalk, then step onto the road to avoid the tree, and then step back onto the dusty sidewalk to avoid the oncoming traffic. It was all second nature to me now, and I did it unthinkingly, my mind wandering, my eyes alert but sometimes unseeing.

This strange woman I did see. And I could see that the dust and the scraps on the street were just being swept from one side to the other, without much cleaning being accomplished. At one point she stopped and broke into a song, using the long handle of the broom like a microphone.

"Who on earth is this woman?" I whispered to Vandana, my school mate who was just about catching up with me.

"Oh, she's the new sweeper woman, who's been employed by the Municipality. I hear she's quite mad."

"Then why employ her?"

"Some sort of initiative to help underprivileged women. My mother said that the Women's Society was adamant that they help battered, abused and disabled women."

I knew that Mrs Mehta, the wife of the Neighbourhood Association's (NA's) chairman was a part of the 'WomSoc', as they called themselves. No doubt she'd pushed the agenda through. How our streets would be any cleaner with this strange woman doing the honours, I couldn't even begin to ponder, nor did I have the energy or will to.

"She's nicer than the last one." Vandana whispered back, as though reading my mind.

True enough, I thought. Tapeshwari had done little but smoke her *beedis* [2] and flirt with the vegetable vendor. At least this one made a show of cleaning, however haphazard it was.

As we walked past her, she stopped singing and looked us straight in the face and hissed. Startled, I stepped back. What was wrong with her? She brandished her broom in my face and sashayed away. Alarmed, I asked Vandana, "Did she just hiss at us?"

She shrugged and said, "Oh yes. She's obsessed with that movie about snakes... you know, the one with the snake taking on a woman's form to ensnare the hero... That was the song she was singing as well. Did you not recognise it?"

I shook my head and carried on walking home. This really was a colony of loonies.

"PUJA, WHAT TOOK YOU SO LONG? I WAS STARTING TO GET worried. I nearly came out looking."

I glanced at the clock on the wall. I was only five minutes late.

"Ma, I stopped to chat with Vandana. I'm sorry."

"Don't frighten me like that again. Go wash your hands. Lunch is ready, I've made your favourite *saag paneer*[3]."

Staring at my face in the mirror, I scrubbed my hands, turning the soap over and over between my palms. How many more years of this could I tolerate without breaking? I splashed my face with water and patted it with the little face towel that hung on the rusty hook near the wash basin. It smelt musty and I made a mental note to throw it in the wash soon. Ma seemed to forget such little things these days.

She sat with me as I ate, asking me about school, about my friends, about every little detail of my life, until I felt like a handbag turned inside out and shaken so vigorously that the insides were completely emptied.

"Have you seen the new sweeper woman, Ma? The crazy one? Apparently, Mrs Mehta has employed her to replace Tapeshwari. She is quite mad, you know. She hissed at us today."

"Hissed? What do you mean? Did she threaten you? I'll get Papa to speak to Mr Mehta. She will be removed! How dare she?"

"No, no, Ma. She is harmless. Just a bit loopy. She was copying the actress from that snake movie, that's all."

I now wished that I hadn't mentioned it. All of Ma's

protective instincts had been triggered, and I just hoped she wouldn't make a big fuss when Papa came home in the evening.

"I'm tired Ma. I'll go and lie down for a bit."

"Yes, go rest Puja. I'll clear up here."

I felt guilty leaving all the dishes to her, but somehow, today I wasn't up to it. I needed to close my eyes and go over the things I'd held back from her.

Jasmin and Sunil.

My two best friends. One of whom I had hoped would be more than just a friend someday. Now, it seemed that they felt exactly the same way about each other and I increasingly found myself becoming the third wheel. Unconsciously, in their whispered exchanges, in their stolen glances, in the brushing of their hands, in their leaning in together over a book, they were shutting me out.

It crushed me, but I pretended not to notice. I pretended that things were still "normal" between us. We were still 'The Three Musketeers', the 'Intrepid Trio', the 'Brazen Bandits', inseparable since Kindergarten, weren't we?

Who was I fooling, and for how long?

I MUST'VE FALLEN ASLEEP FOR THE NEXT THING I KNEW, Ma was standing next to me, holding a cup of tea and calling my name.

I sat up, disorientated.

"What time is it?"

"Nearly five o'clock. I thought I'd let you sleep, you looked so tired."

Ma sat beside me as I sipped on my tea. I wished she'd go out as she used to before. She'd had a life... before. Friends she'd go out shopping with, go to the cinema and watch the latest Hindi blockbuster with. Now, home was just us three, and more often than not, just Ma and me. Papa worked progressively longer hours, avoiding the house and avoiding the two other people in it - people who reminded him of the past. A past that had been so happy and full of love, laughter and potential.

"Homework *hai*?⁴"

I nodded. There was always homework, but unlike other students, I didn't find it a nuisance. To me, it was a refuge and an escape. Academically, I had always been strong but lately I had invested so much into my studies that I was miles ahead of everyone in my class. Regularly hailed as 'brilliant', 'gifted' or 'a student par excellence', it was the only thing that brought me any fulfilment.

Papa came home at nine o'clock, long after I had finished my homework, eaten my dinner and watched my favourite Television serial. He lowered himself into the armchair with a sigh as I glanced up from my book. Ma had taken his briefcase and brought him a glass of water. They would eat together as she never ate without him.

"What are you reading, Puja?" Papa asked, feigning interest.

"Oh, just a book Jasmin lent me. Some horror thing she really enjoyed."

"Where is Jasmin these days? I haven't seen her in a while. She used to come around so often..."

There was an unasked question in there and I couldn't bring myself to answer it.

I looked back at my book, mildly vexed. I wanted to ask him why none of his friends visited anymore either. Why he didn't have his *taash*⁵ parties, with whiskey and chicken *tangdi*⁶ from the local *dhaba.*⁷ Why, instead, he made excuses to leave home early and return as late as possible. Why he wouldn't meet Ma's eyes when she asked him a question and desperately demanded a reply. Why?

I said nothing.

MY PERIOD STARTED THE NEXT MORNING. THERE WAS A little stain on my nightie and with a groan I washed it hurriedly, knowing that precious minutes lost here could mean I'd miss my school bus. Shovelling in my breakfast toast, I brushed my hair with ferocity, trying not to choke. Only momentarily I paused, as another, familiar reflection swam into view in the mirror and disappeared just as quickly. I tied my hair in a ponytail, kissed Ma on the cheek and ran to the bus stop.

Vandana and I stood together at the back of the school bus. Every time the bus went over a pothole we were jostled together.

"Did you hear about Mrs Ratnani?"

"No?"

"Her son is bringing home a British girlfriend and she has taken to her bed."

"What do you mean? Is she unwell?"

Vandana gave me a look.

"No, it's all *nautanki*[8]. She is such a drama queen. She'll have the *Angrez* [9]fleeing before you know it. She wants a nice, Indian *gharelu bahu* [10]for her son. None of this foreign nonsense!"

"But surely, it's his choice who he marries? If he loves this girl..."

"Love shmove! Puja, open your eyes. All this only happens in the movies. In real life, we marry the person our family chooses for us. You should know better..."

She bit her lip and looked away guiltily.

My eyes filled with tears that I determinedly blinked away. I would give no one the satisfaction of knowing just how deep my wound was.

. . .

JASMIN AND SUNIL STOOD TOGETHER, SLIGHTLY APART FROM the rest of the class. They both looked up at the same time and smiled at me, beckoning me over. I went and stood next to them.

"Assembly is going to be loooong today." Jasmin groaned.

"Why?"

"Some visitor from France who wants to tell us how wonderful we are."

Sunil laughed and chipped in. "We just saw him walking alongside Mrs Padhi. She seemed really engrossed in conversation with him. Of course, as he's a *gora*,[11] she wants to impress him, *na*[12]?"

Once or twice a week we had international visitors who were so taken by our school that they insisted on giving us long, rambling lectures about the differences between Indian and Western schooling. We always triumphed in terms of education, discipline and respect for our teachers, according to them. Since most of us just dozed through these assemblies, we seemed like a particularly docile lot. If only they knew the nicknames we had for our teachers, or the shenanigans we got up to when no one was looking. But I suppose in comparison to our Western contemporaries, we were still pretty tame.

A short while later I examined the pattern the coir mat had left on my left thigh. As predicted, the assembly had been going on forever. I'd gone from sitting cross-legged, to changing positions several times over. It didn't help that all four hundred of us had to sit on the large coir mat laid out on the floor of our assembly hall, whilst the teachers and the esteemed visitors were comfortably seated on the chairs lined up on the periphery of the large hall.

"Can you imagine *Chhipkali*[13] trying to haul her arse off the floor?" Jasmin giggled behind her hand, reading my mind and my mutinous scowl directed at the chairs.

Chhipkali was the moniker we had christened our vile Chemistry teacher with. Someone had once commented on how she resembled a fat, ugly lizard with her long chin and her habit of sticking her tongue out unexpectedly. That description had stuck. She didn't help herself by only ever wearing brown, her favourite colour, and so for all intents and purposes, she became *Chhipkali* to us.

I chuckled in response, quickly transitioning into a fit of coughs as I caught *Chhipkali's* imperious gaze. It wouldn't do to piss her off this early in the morning.

At lunch time we sat together and shared our sandwiches. I watched Sunil tease Jasmin with a little lump in my throat.

"Stop eating jam sandwiches. All your teeth will fall out by the time you're eighteen, you fatso!"

Jasmin gave him a dimpled smile and retorted smartly, "*You* stop eating ham sandwiches. All your good *karma* will evaporate by the time you're eighteen, you carnivore!"

I wandered off to the library. I doubted they even noticed me leave.

VANDANA AND I WALKED TOGETHER FROM THE BUS STOP IN silence. I hadn't forgiven her throwaway remark this morning and she tried apologising in a roundabout way.

"Mummy is making *gujias*[14] today. Should I bring some to school for you tomorrow?"

I half-smiled at her attempts to make it up to me. Oh, what the heck!

"Yes, that'll be lovely Vandy. Thank you."

I'd inadvertently used my childhood nickname for her and quickly glanced over to see if she'd noticed. There was a time when our families had been close, and Vandy had been like a little sister to me. That was before, of course.

She nudged me hard in my ribs and said, "Look, look!"

Our crazy sweeper woman was up to her usual antics. This time she'd propped her broom against the boundary wall of the police colony flats. She was sitting right next to the broom, her back to the wall, with two broken buckets in front of her, and was banging on them loudly, singing off key. An empty Thums-up bottle rolled on the ground next to her, almost in rhythm with her discordant singing. A crowd had gathered at a distance watching her performance with astonished glee. Some children jumped up and down squealing, "Paagal[15], paagal..."

Vandy and I stood quietly, away from the crowd. We waited to see how long her rendition of this popular song would last. Not long, as it turned out, for a stone came whizzing past us and smacked her right in the centre of her forehead with a resounding crack. She collapsed to the ground, clutching her head, groaning terribly.

"Who did that?!" I swung ferociously towards the rapidly dispersing group, feeling the rage spread through my body, my heart hammering hard against my rib cage. "Who did it?"

Unsurprisingly, no one owned up. People started shuffling off and the children looked scared and backed away from me.

"Bunch of cowards!" I muttered as I moved to join Vandy who was already by the woman's side, lifting her off the ground and sitting her upright.

Blood was trickling into her eye and I unsuccessfully attempted to use my handkerchief to stem the flow. Vandy meanwhile was knocking on the nearest door, shouting for assistance.

Onir, the writer chap, came out looking annoyed. His kurta [16]was rumpled and his nose twitched even more than usual. With the sparse whiskers on his chin, the teeth he could barely contain behind his thin lips and that twitchy nose, he never failed to remind me of a rodent, the kind that infested the garbage facility on the outskirts of the locality.

"What's all this noise? Can't even get a decent nap in this neighbourhood!"

"She needs help! She's bleeding, some idiot threw a stone and hit her."

He glared at a frantic Vandy, and then at the woman and me huddled together.

"Wait!" He went retreated into his house grumpily, re-emerging a little while later with some cotton wool, antiseptic solution and a bottle of water.

"She's filthy! We need to wash the wound first."

The woman cowered as he approached her. She started trembling and hitting her head, getting more agitated as he came closer.

"*Uff*, what is wrong with her?! I wouldn't touch her with a barge pole if my life depended on it! Here, you girls do it. Return the stuff to me once you've finished."

He strode home, muttering under his breath and shut the door with a bang.

"What an arrogant so-and-so!" Vandy spat out as she poured the water on my kerchief.

"Yeah, but a helpful one. Must be the moody, artistic type."

I washed the woman's wound gently and then used the antiseptic solution to wipe it. She flinched, then shut her eyes as I tended to her wound.

"*Aapka naam kya hai*? What is your name?"

She still had her eyes shut as she muttered, "Lakshmi."

We accompanied Lakshmi into her little makeshift hut at the end of the street. There a little mat on the floor, a bundle of what looked like clothes in the corner and two pots that sat by an old kerosene stove. We barely managed to fit into the small and ramshackle structure, but we settled her on to the mat, asking if she needed anything else. She just closed her eyes and lay there quietly. Vandy and I looked at each other helplessly. There wasn't much more we could do, so we left her and went to return Onir's stuff to him.

It saddened me to see how little this woman possessed. Poverty manifests itself in various ways in this world - some are poor of money, others of love, of attention, of good health, or of peace of mind. Lakshmi seemed to be poor of everything.

THERE WAS A LOW HANGING MIST, AND THE WORLD SEEMED almost sepia-toned, as though all colour had been leached out of it. She was sitting on a bench and reading from a book, but the book was upside down. I kept trying to straighten it, but she'd snatch it away, laughing as she did.

"Why *didi*[17]?" I started to cry.

"Because I had to." She looked at me solemnly and then, quietly evaporated.

I woke up, my heart thudding. It was still dark outside. I peered at my watch. It was 4:30 am. I shut my eyes, trying to go back to sleep, but the dream kept revisiting me. How real it had seemed! Unable to sleep, I got out of bed and quietly made my way to the balcony.

I'd spent many a morning here, communing with God. It was strange how I always felt His presence at this quiet hour, as if all the clamouring voices had finally shut up, and He was listening to me. Only me.

Sitting on the wicker chair I contemplated life. How one small decision could lead to unforeseen consequences, and one big decision could upend everything. There were so many questions I had for my God, my invisible companion of the hour, but I refrained from asking any, knowing that our misery was nothing in comparison to what millions suffered everyday. So, I asked him nothing.

In the stillness of that early morning, waiting for dawn to fill the inky sky with a burst of orange, I retreated into myself for a while. No thoughts were allowed to penetrate my meditation, I just concentrated on breathing in and breathing out. After a while, I noticed a pinprick of light in the distance and peered at it. Lakshmi was up early. Maybe she couldn't sleep either. I wondered about her - where she had come from, what her past had been like, why she was the way she was. I made a mental note to check on her.

Slowly, the world started to wake up.

Birds started chirping, and a little sparrow came and sat on the railing, cocking its head from one side to another, wondering perhaps if there were any *chapatti* [18]crumbs for him. Our local *subziwaala*[19] started making his rounds, calling out to the housewives to come and purchase the fresh vegetables on his *thela*[20]. Tightly rolled copies of 'The Times of India', 'The Indian Express' and 'The Hindustan Times' came flying into people's verandahs and balconies, thrown by the practised hands of the newspaper*wallah*.[21] Maids rushed to buy milk from the milk booth. All the hustle and bustle of everyday life signalled the start of a new day.

Papa came on to the balcony with his cup of coffee, the only one he allowed himself in a day. He had acquired a taste for it when posted down South, much before he had married Ma. It was she who had put two and two together, forbidding him more than a cup, that too, only in the morning, and cured him of his hitherto unexplained insomnia.

"How long have you been sitting here?" He picked up the rolled newspaper, giving me a sidelong glance.

"A couple of hours."

"Couldn't sleep?"

"Nightmare."

"Hmmm."

We sat in silence. Papa flicked through the newspaper, sipping his coffee, while I tried observing him undetected.

He had lost a lot of hair in the last two years, and what remained was greying rapidly. His face was gaunt and his eyes seemed perpetually haunted. Two lines ran perpendicular to his mouth on either side and he rarely smiled. I wondered if I would see the jovial, fun loving man that he had once been, ever again. I doubted it.

Ma came outside with a cup of tea and handed it to me silently. On mornings like these, hardly any words were exchanged, but we all knew what the other was thinking. We sat together, each of us busy in our thoughts, bound together by blood, by love and by that unspoken thing that always hovered at the edges of our consciousness.

"I BROUGHT THE *GUJIAS*." VANDY HAD PUSHED THROUGH the crowd on the school bus towards me. She handed me a little package.

"Did aunty ask who it was for?" I didn't want her to get into trouble. Not over this, not over me.

"She knew." She looked at my face searchingly then said, "Puja, it was you who stopped coming over. We never told you to. We wanted to help... we offered to..."

"Please don't!" I thrust the package back in her hands and elbowed my way to the front of the bus.

The younger children looked at me curiously. I held on to the handrail, steadfastly refusing to meet anyone's eyes. Curiosity! That's all they'd ever had. Curiosity and gossip. *Did you hear? Can you believe it? I always knew!* It sickened me. Our loss had been incomprehensible; unbelievable. All it had become was fodder, grist to the rumour-mongering mill. I'd be damned if I fed another word into it!

. . .

"They are auditioning for the Annual day production today."

"Why so early?" I asked, mystified, as I knew the performance wouldn't be till November.

"Someone major is coming to see it! I don't know who, but it's going to be a very big production." Jasmin practically squealed this at me.

Jasmin was excited, she really hoped to land a main part. I was content to dress up as a tree and stand in the background. Sunil, on the other hand, was terrified by the whole ordeal.

"I will NOT do it. I'm telling you, I'll be sick for the next three months and not come to school at all. I refuse to participate in some stupid dance!"

Sunil's fear wasn't unjustified. In the past six months he'd shot up and filled out. His boyish features were starting to look manly, and at nearly six feet tall, he towered over even the senior boys. It was therefore inevitable that he would be a candidate for the lead male role.

"Relax", I muttered to him. "I'm sure they'll pick someone else. Just do your absolute worst when you audition."

Somewhat relieved at my conjecture, he followed us reluctantly into the assembly hall.

Mrs Bindra, our dance teacher, was a tiny, stick-like woman who had the ability to reduce any man, woman or child to a gibbering mess. Her huge eyes, mesmerising and beautiful as they were during dance performances, were equally effective at quelling any kind of opposition or disobedience. Her rows with the other teachers were the stuff of legends. If a student got roped into any kind of dance performance, they could only hope the rehearsals didn't clash with any important lessons; rehearsals always

prevailed over academics, studies be damned! Bindra
brooked no opposition.

I WASN'T THE ONLY ONE WHO HAD BEEN TAKEN BY SURPRISE
by the early auditions. As Jasmin had said, word on the street
was that we were expecting a very special guest for the show,
meaning that Bindra had gone into overdrive and wanted
everything in place before we broke up for the holidays. We'd
launch straight into rehearsals as soon as the new school year
commenced.

Right now, she was feverishly auditioning boys and girls
for the parts that hadn't been filled. Bindra's bunch sat haugh-
tily around her, commenting amongst themselves, whispering
the occasional tidbit into her ear. Most of the major roles had
been handed out to them already, much before the auditions
had become official news.

"Priya Majumdar in the lead, as expected!" Jas exclaimed,
disgust written all over her face.

"She is a wonderful dancer Jas, and so pretty too!"

"Yeah, but what about the rest of us? When will we ever
get a chance?"

"Look, it's her final year. Once she passes out of school,
opportunities will come your way too."

"Oh, come on! You know Bindra. The next tier of
favourites have already been lined up. She thinks I'm too
moti[22] to be graceful."

"You're not fat! And grace has nothing to do with weight.
You are an extremely graceful dancer. Don't put yourself
down this way..."

"Not like Ambika *didi*! My goodness, she was a dream to
watch. So incredibly beautiful too! Priya isn't a patch on her."

Jasmin had said it unthinkingly, truthfully even, but I
couldn't help the tears that pooled in my eyes. I dug my nails

into my hand to stop them from spilling over. She looked at my face and went pale.

"Oh my God, I'm so sorry. I'm so, so sorry."

I shook my head and looked away. It was kind of her to remember my sister this way. I knew there was no malice in what she had said, but dammit! Why couldn't I manage my emotions better?

Someone prodded me with a finger.

"Look, it's Sunil. She's called him up..."

Jasmin reached out and took my hand. She gave it a little squeeze and I squeezed back.

"THAT WAS JUST PLAIN MEAN!"

We were walking together to the classroom. I was still too shaken to comment, but Jasmin was doing all the raving and ranting on my behalf. Even Sunil, mightily miffed after having performed the worst and *still* getting picked for the lead role, was nodding along in sympathy.

"How could she do that?! She knows full well that Puja has never been interested in dance. How could she say those things to her? Comparing her to Ambika *didi*! Calling her wooden and expressionless. Who the hell does she think she is? I'm going to Mrs Padhi to complain!" Jasmin was livid.

Mrs Padhi was our Principal, and I very much doubted that she would do anything. She was just as intimidated by Mrs Bindra as the rest of the faculty.

"That was *baaad*, really bad. Especially after what happened to Ambika *didi*. She had no right to bring up her name this way." Sunil rarely got involved in arguments but I could tell from the slow way that he pronounced his words that he was seething. Not just at Bindra's casual cruelty towards me, but also at making him look like an effete idiot by slotting him into a dance-drama he had tried his hardest to sidestep. "She'd better watch out! I'm going to make her life hell in rehearsals."

THAT AFTERNOON I WALKED FASTER THAN USUAL FROM THE bus stop. The plan was to avoid Vandana as I had done for the last two years, using the same tactics as always. I didn't care for the curiosity in her eyes, or the sympathy in her words. Our pain was ours alone. Nothing anyone said or did would change that.

It was a particularly hot afternoon with the temperature hitting 40 degrees celsius. I stopped to take a quick glug from my water bottle when I heard the scream. Before I could even turn, a figure ran past me, broom in hand, yelling, "*Haraamzaada! Saala! Kutta!*[23] *Teri toh...*"

Lakshmi was raining blows on a young man whose bicycle had fallen to the side. The choicest of *gaalis* [24]spewed out of her mouth. Vandana stood next to her, open-mouthed, mirroring my own astonishment. The noise was enough to draw Onir out, novel in hand, glasses perched on his nose, looking irritated.

"What's this *tamasha* [25]now? Something every day!"

We walked over to the commotion. More people were gathering around and sniggering at the man's plight. Finally, Vandana put her hand on Lakshmi's arm, urging her to stop. She tucked her broom away and spat on the man.

"What is all this, huh? Always creating a problem!" Onir was glaring at Lakshmi who refused to meet his eyes. The young man was straightening his cycle, ready to be on his way.

"One minute!" Vandana stood in front of him. "Say sorry to me. Say it. Now!"

"Sorry *behenji*[26]. *Maaf kar do*[27]." He folded his palms together, sweat dripping off his brow.

Indignation and fury mixed together in her voice as Vandy stared him down. "*Phir kisi ladki ko aise chheda toh dekhna...!*[28]" Little Vandy had quite a temper on her when provoked.

He pedalled away without a backward glance.

"What happened?" I asked her quietly.

"He pinched my bottom while cycling past. Gave me such a shock that I screamed. Then Lakshmi came running with her broom..." She shrugged. I knew the rest already.

Onir was saying something to Lakshmi, who was uncharacteristically subdued. We went up to them. He looked at us, frowned and walked away.

"Lakshmi, what you did was very brave," I patted her back, "But it was also foolhardy. The boy could've had a knife. He could come back with *gundas*[29] and attack you. Please be careful next time. Don't hit people with your broom."

"She did it to protect me," Vandana said. I could hear the tremor in her voice. The anger had given way to distress.

"Yes, I know. Come, let's walk her back to her hut."

THE SUMMER HOLIDAYS WERE FAST APPROACHING AND I knew Ma wanted us to go back to Darjeeling. It had been our annual retreat. The little cottage had been bequeathed to her by her spinster aunt, and every year, without fail, the four of us would leave Delhi in the month of June to enjoy the cooler climes of Darjeeling. We hadn't gone the last two years.

"Anuj, I need to check if the cottage is okay or not. It's been locked up for so long. We have to go this year."

"Then you go Meera. Take Puja with you. I can't leave, there's just too much work."

It was the same feeble excuse he'd been using for the last two years.

"Papa, please come. I know..." I stopped to weigh my

words, then continued softly, "I know it won't be the same without *didi*, but please..."

This was the first time I'd addressed him in this manner, and I noted his surprise. We never spoke of *didi*. Each of us held our pain and guilt close to our hearts. Each of us knew that the others were hurting. Yet, not once in the last two years had we ever talked about what really happened, and why.

Ma went up to him and laid her head on his shoulder, not saying a word. He looked at me, his expression unfathomable. Then he nodded slowly and called me over. I nestled into the crook of his arm and let my tears fall to the ground silently.

THERE HAD BEEN A TIME WHEN WE'D BEEN HAPPY. A TIME when our house was always filled with people and laughter, and at the centre of it all was my beautiful sister. She was six years older than me, and the life and soul of the household. A second mother to me, a confidante for Ma, and Papa's favourite child, Ambika *didi* could do no wrong. Until she did.

Falling pregnant at the age of nineteen, with the father refusing to take responsibility, this was every average Indian household's most dreaded nightmare. A boyfriend who escaped to America for 'further studies', a younger sister who knew of his existence but never breathed a word to her parents, a mother so caught up in her social whirl that she didn't see her daughter's heart breaking, and a father so trenchant in his orthodox views that telling him the truth would have been worse than bearing the consequences alone.

Had Ambika *didi* spoken to any of us, would things have turned out differently? Had she communicated her dilemma, would we have understood and supported her? These were the questions that still plagued us, day and night. There would never be any answers as the one person who could provide them, was gone forever.

———————————————

1. Loose shirt and pants ensemble, commonly worn in North India
2. A type of cheap cigarette made of unprocessed tobacco wrapped in leaves.
3. Spinach with Indian cheese
4. Signifying "is there?"
5. Playing cards
6. Drumsticks
7. Cheap and cheerful eatery
8. Overacting
9. Brit
10. Domesticated wife
11. White man
12. No?
13. Lizard
14. Sweet deep-fried dumpling
15. Crazy person
16. Loose shirt
17. Elder sister
18. Indian flatbread
19. Vegetable seller
20. Barrow
21. Newspaper delivery man
22. Fat
23. Abusive terms in Hindi
24. Abuse
25. Commotion
26. Sister-like
27. Please forgive me
28. Don't you dare molest a girl ever again!
29. Hooligans

II

Darjeeling had stirred up so many memories at first, it seemed unthinkable that we would derive any joy at all from this vacation. Yet, slowly we had loosened up. Without the daily constraints of job, school and household chores we had learned to relax in each others' company. Once or twice Ma had pointed out a particular spot that *didi* had liked walking to. Papa had smiled sadly, and my heart hadn't clenched in its usual way.

Did this mean we were 'moving on' as friends and family had advised us to? No! We could never move on. We could never fill that huge, gaping hole in our lives. What did they know? These everyday messiahs who preached fate, destiny and acceptance. What did they know what it felt like to have your heart wrenched out of your chest and be replaced with a leaden rock? What it felt like waking up each morning to find your pillow case drenched with tears. How every single happy memory became a taunt, a jibe. How every joyful moment came tinged with guilt.

The fact that we could not even articulate our pain to each other, meant there would never be any 'moving on'.

After all, moving on required acknowledgement, and we were still living in denial.

Still, there were quiet moments of contentment. Nature soothed our wounds in ways that we could not explain. The verdant hills, the colourful blossoms, the tea gardens, the quaint little houses, the people - simple, smiling, welcoming, provided the very respite our bruised souls needed. No one was judging us here. We were just ordinary people amongst other ordinary people going about their daily lives, and there was a strange comfort in that.

The mundane acts of cleaning the cottage together, buying groceries from the little shop down the road, sitting and drinking our *chai*[1] in companionable silence, knit us back together as a family.

Papa tuned the old transistor radio to the channel that played music from the 50's, the "most melodious era of Hindi films", as he had claimed many a time before. I would catch him exchanging glances with Ma when a favourite song came on. It soothed me to know that there were still remnants of affection between them. That all the cruel, bitter words they had spoken to each other hadn't been entirely serious. That if there was some love between them, there must be a little for me too.

WHEN SCHOOL REOPENED IN JULY, I FELT READY TO FACE the likes of Bindra. The only armour against cruelty is the indifference that comes from a place of complete security. Our vacation had provided me with a semblance of it, an elusive knowledge that there was still a life to be lived, however painful it would be.

As for Jasmin and Sunil, I could see how much better suited they were to one another than I could have ever been in a coupling. My temperament, my independence, my need for hibernation, and now, the history of my household, made me eminently unsuitable as a romantic attachment. Maybe I had always suspected that I would stay single. *Didi*'s fate had only reinforced this belief.

With these thoughts swirling through my head, I walked to the bus stop, barely noticing the morning activity around me. When we first moved into this colony twelve years ago, it had been a quiet suburban outpost. Back then, if I craned my neck, I could see fields in the distance. Occasionally, the smell of manure would waft over to us. This was a quiet locality and not much happened around here. Our neighbours were mostly office workers or owners of small businesses, all middle class people, working hard at their livelihoods. Children played together, women shopped together, and the men met up for their occasional *taash*[2] parties. There was a sense of community and a feeling of belonging. No one person stood out as having too much or too little. 'Rich' was a description reserved for others. Here, we were proud of our Bajaj scooters and Royal Enfield motorcycles. Owning a car was unheard of, and if, by some stroke of luck or providence, you did end up with one, well that was upward mobility!

The Sahnis were an ordinary family, just like us. When they'd moved in next door, Ma had gone over with a plate of homemade *barfi*[3] to welcome them. She'd come home ecstatic at having found a soul-sister in Yamini Sahni. I was just five, but I remember Ma telling *didi*, "Rajat is only a year older. You can tie him a *raakhi*[4] next year. Yamini won't mind. She is so lovely!"

As two sisters with no male cousins in our vicinity, *Raksha Bandhan*[5] was a festival that we were unable to participate in. *Didi* felt this keenly. She too, had wanted a brother on whose wrist she could tie a colourful band, and in return, get the assurance of protection, with some money thrown in as a gift. I suspect it was more the lure of the lucre, than any other aspect of *Raksha Bandhan* that she really missed out on. Now, Ma was presenting her with the next best solution, how could she refuse?

Didi did tie him a *raakhi* the next couple of years, but as the Sahni's wealth and social standing increased, so did their aloofness towards their less fortunate neighbours. Oh, Mrs Sahni would invite all the neighbourhood children to watch movies on their newly acquired Video Cassette Recorder, but it was always with an air of 'Lady Bountiful'. I had never bought into the Sahni myth, and I could tell that *didi* too was reluctant to continue the *raakhi* brother charade any longer.

Ma was not easily convinced. This was her only way into the Sahni's enchanted circle, that she was increasingly being left out of. She still clung to the belief that Yamini was just really busy, not really ignoring her, had too many social obligations that Mr Sahni saddled her with. They were soul-sisters after all. Hadn't she introduced her to her favourite *saree wallah*[6]? Hadn't they gone grocery shopping on multiple occasions? Hadn't she sent the *kaamwaali bai*[7] over when their own maid hadn't turned up?

It was Papa who finally snapped the tenuous link when he had an almighty row with Mr Sahni. With our water pressure running low for many days, one morning he decided to investigate why the newly installed bore-well pump wasn't doing its job. That's when he discovered that Mr Sahni had paid some lackey to attach a sideline to siphon more water to their side. All hell broke loose, and we never spoke to the Sahnis again. Or so we thought.

THE FIRST FEW DAYS OF A NEW SCHOOL YEAR WERE ALL about settling in. Teachers introduced themselves to us. Some we were pleased to have and others whose reputation preceded them, not so much. Sadly, *Chhipkali* was still very much on our timetable, but we also had Miss De Cruz, the lovely English teacher, and Mrs Chugh, the Maths teacher who could edify even the nincompoops. All in all, it wasn't a bad line up. It could have been worse.

The seating arrangements, however, were a disaster! Jasmin, Sunil and I had been put in three different corners of the classroom, in a deliberate attempt to split us up. As my scores had been consistently at the top, I could only imagine it was to get the two of them to pull up their socks. After all, we were preparing for the Class Ten Board Examinations, and although neither of them was stupid, their performance thus far had been average at best. The teachers accredited it to excessive chatting during lessons. I suspected the first flush of love.

I still felt a tinge of disquiet when I saw Jasmin and Sunil together, but I was coming to terms with it. Nothing, not even their burgeoning romance, could wreck our friendship. I had experienced loss, seen how life could change in a matter of seconds, and I refused to lose anyone else I cared for, if I could help it.

"How was Darjeeling?" Jasmin asked after a lengthy moan about *Chhipkali*.

"Good! Yeah, really good." I was surprised at how honestly I could say this, but a delayed pang of guilt still hit me, and I looked down at my hands. *Didi* hadn't been there. How could I still have had a good time? Jasmin hadn't noticed. She prattled on about the cousins from Kanpur who'd landed up for the entire vacation, and how she'd been displaced from her room, and had to spend the entire Summer camped out on the sofa. Something she'd said must've been funny because Sunil started laughing. I joined in politely.

"So, you're about to start rehearsals soon?" Jasmin liked needling Sunil, and this was a particularly sore subject.

"You wait…", he grinned evilly, "Bindra won't know what's hit her…"

"What are you plotting?" I asked, a sense of unease growing in the pit of my stomach. It never boded well to cross Bindra.

"Never you mind. All I will say is that it will be perfect. A night to remember!"

AUGUST WAS A MURKY MONTH - HOT, STICKY AND WET. The humidity and the weather irritated me. I could never be one of those children who danced in the rain, being far too fastidious for it. *Didi,* on the other hand, had loved the monsoon season. She used to ask me to come on to the balcony to smell the wet earth. She said it smelt like something primeval, as though through this one smell we could be connected to those that came before us, and those who would follow. For unlike us, Nature was constant. I nearly always raised my eyebrows at her and scoffed at her fancies.

Today, however, as I walked home, I inhaled deeply and thought back to all those moments that I had taken for granted. How careless we are with the people we love! We assume that they will be around us always, that their love will surround and cocoon us for an eternity. We assume that we are the centre of the Universe and forget that others have their own internal lives, oftentimes at odds with our own truths. We believe that we will go on forever, bound to each other through our familial ties. We believe we are indestructible. Perhaps that is the only way to live - to never actually think about death.

VANDANA HADN'T BEEN TO SCHOOL THE LAST FEW DAYS, and I had missed her easy company on the way to and from the bus stop. Although neither of us were ready to repair the frayed threads of our old friendship yet, a certain tension between us had dissipated. I was even considering taking up her invitation to visit.

Just as I pondered this, the skies opened up in a sudden downpour. The rainstorm had an unexpected violence to it. It wanted to drench everything and everyone in its deluge and through the thunder that rumbled ominously, to the lightning that crackled across the sky, it declared its intent. This was no five-minute cloudburst. This was torrential rain and it was here to stay.

I took shelter under the awning of a house. Stupidly having forgotten my umbrella at home, I'd have to wait it out. People were rushing past, holding plastic bags over their heads, hiking their *sarees* or trousers up, past their ankles. The smart ones who had brought their umbrellas were nevertheless finding them useless against the gale force winds and the rain pelting at them sideways. Drains, unable to handle the volume or velocity of the rain, had already started to overflow.

In all of this mayhem, I glimpsed a hand waving at me. Lakshmi! She was calling me towards her, urging me to take shelter in her hut. I didn't need to think twice as I ran out.

Inside her little hut, I noticed that the two pots had been placed strategically to catch the leaks from her roof. She handed me an old cloth to wipe myself with while she busied herself make tea on her stove. I observed how neat everything in the hut was. She seemed to have gathered a few more belongings. A rickety chair, a small pedestal fan plugged into a dodgy, stolen electrical outlet, a picture of Lord Krishna torn off an old calendar and a moth eaten blanket. People's charity knew no bounds.

I observed her straining the tea into two steel tumblers and noted that she looked well. Her cheeks had filled out and she seemed to have an air of contentment. She turned to me smiling and offered me the *chai*. I took it and blew into the tumbler, taking a tentative sip.

"*Shukriya*[8]." I thanked her, sitting on the chair as she indicated. She squatted next to me, drinking her own tea.

"*Woh doosri ladki?*[9]"

I told her Vandana had been ill. She nodded, clicking her tongue sympathetically. I looked at her closely. Something had changed. She didn't seem as unhinged as usual.

"*Aap theek ho?*[10]" I hoped that my concern didn't come across as fraudulent.

"*Haan*[11]," She smiled, patting her stomach, "*Pet se hoon.*[12]"

The news of Lakshmi's pregnancy hit me like a thunderbolt. For some bizarre reason, it brought the entirety of *didi's* saga rushing back. There were no parallels between the two of them - Lakshmi was poor, mentally deficient and happy to have this baby despite her straitened circumstances, while *didi* had been unhappy, secretive and desperate, despite all her other advantages. I sat dumbstruck for a while, and then overcome by a strange protective instinct, reassured Lakshmi that all would be well, before running out into the rain and all the way home.

MA WAS WORKING THROUGH MY SODDEN LOCKS WITH A hairdryer, clucking all the while about the rain and the mess it had made everywhere. The roads had all but disappeared underwater, and all sorts of debris, from plastic bags to someone's old shoe, floated past the house. I was still debating how to break the news to her when she announced quite suddenly, "The WomSoc ladies came by today."

"Oh?" My curiosity was piqued in spite of myself. I loathed Mrs Mehta. I'd always felt that her charity was self-serving. Had she been truly charitable, she would have been supportive in our hour of need. Instead, we had been avoided like the plague.

"They are doing a charity drive for that sweeper woman. You know, that mad one?"

"What for?" For a second I wondered if they already knew.

"Well, it's come to their attention that she has very little by way of possessions and they want to try and help her. Once winter arrives, the poor woman will freeze to death in the little hut. They are trying to collect woollens, *razais*, utensils etc."

"How nice of them!"

Ma narrowed her eyes at me. "None of that sarcasm from you, young lady! This is a good thing they are doing, never mind the reasons."

"Ohhh! So, there is an underlying reason?"

"Well, Mr Mehta wants to stand for the local elections later this year."

"And this sort of charitable drive will just bolster his standing, won't it?"

"It's the end result that counts, and if the poor woman is getting the help she needs, then why not?"

"She's pregnant." I pronounced this slowly, looking straight at my mother in the dressing table mirror.

The colour drained from her face and she sank down on the bed, hairdryer falling to the floor.

"Who? How...?"

"I don't know Ma, I really don't. But if those hyenas find out, they'll run her out of the locality. It might be one of the men in our colony and if she opens her mouth, he's done for."

PAPA, MA AND I PAID LAKSHMI A VISIT THE SAME EVENING.

Papa had been reluctant but we had persuaded him it would be for the best.

"Lakshmi, *hum andar aa sakte hain*[13]?"

She opened the makeshift door and glowered at Papa.

"He's my father Lakshmi. He's safe."

She allowed us in reluctantly. I could sense that she was in a bad mood, but the situation had to be addressed quickly or it could escalate beyond control.

Ma gave her the old shawl she had brought with her. It wasn't much but Lakshmi's eyes lit up. She had probably never owned something as beautiful as this in her life. She kept stroking the material as if to reassure herself that it was hers now.

"Lakshmi, I told my parents about your... ummm... condition. They want to help."

She kept stroking the shawl, refusing to look up.

Ma spoke softly. "*Bachcha kiska hai?*[14] Who is the father?"

There was a moment's silence before she looked up.

"*Bhagwan ka hai*[15]."

Papa and Ma exchanged glances. This wasn't going well. Papa spoke up.

"We want to help you Lakshmi. You need to get checked by a doctor and you need to stay in a proper place. There is a women's shelter we could take you to."

Lakshmi began to shake violently. She started hitting her head and moaning.

"*Nahin, nahin. Main nahin jaoongi.*[16].."

It took a while for her to calm down, with us muttering assurances and exchanging worried looks amongst ourselves. Clearly, whisking her out of this hut was not an option. Getting any straight answers was also proving difficult, till Ma hit upon a strategy.

"What will you name the baby?"

"Krishna."

"And if it's a girl?"

"Krishna."

"That is a beautiful name. I see you have a picture of Lord Krishna on your wall. Would you like a little statue for your *mandir*[17] too?"

Lakshmi nodded and smiled shyly at my mother. She reached forward and stroked Ma's cheek.

"*Aap bahut sundar ho*[18]."

I HAD NEVER REALLY REFLECTED ON THE FACT THAT MY mother was a beautiful woman. She wasn't glamorous like Yamini Sahni, nor was she drop dead gorgeous like the then-reigning actress Rekha. Hers was a subtle beauty. It lay in the symmetry of her features, in her almond shaped eyes, in her fair complexion, her tiny rosebud mouth and her thick hair that she looped into a bun at the base of her neck. *Didi* had inherited all this and Papa's long, strong limbs. No wonder people used to say "*nazar na lag jaye*[19]". The evil eye had fallen upon her regardless.

"She seems to have suffered some trauma at the women's shelter. Maybe that's why she's adamant she doesn't want to leave."

Ma and Papa were sitting alongside each other on the sofa back home, discussing Lakshmi, while I ate the grapes Ma had placed in a bowl, half heartedly skimming through a magazine.

"But Meera, how can she carry on living in that hut? Besides, how do we know she's even safe there? If whoever impregnated her finds out..."

"Anuj, she's hardly bandying his name about, is she? She's claiming God's given her the baby."

"... and her mental state! Is she even capable of bringing a child up?"

As they argued and discussed Lakshmi, I felt a sudden hollowness at the pit of my stomach. Would they have been quite as nonchalant about *didi's* pregnancy?

"I think we need to leave her where she is. She's happy there, so why move her? We can keep an eye on her. And Papa, maybe you could discreetly suggest to Mr Mehta that if the WomSoc are seen to be helping Lakshmi in her condition, he might win more votes."

Ma and Papa looked at me as I pronounced this. There was a glint in Papa's eye that I hadn't seen in a while. A sense of purpose combined with a streak of mischief. I had a sudden glimpse of the man he used to be, one who loved pranks and April Fool's jokes. He couldn't wait to massage Mr Mehta's enormous ego and have him turn to putty in his hands.

Ma came over to where I was sitting and patted my head.

"When did you become this wise, my little one?"

REHEARSALS WERE NOT GOING WELL. SUNIL KEPT stumbling over his own feet, crashing into Priya and generally making a nuisance of himself. Bindra was just about reining her temper in the hope that she could transform him into some semblance of a dancer. It was very entertaining to watch.

Jasmin was giggling when Bindra's gaze fell upon her.

"You! Yes you, fatso... what's so funny? Are you here to rehearse or to laugh? Stand up!"

Jasmin stood up. Bindra was glaring at her, but behind her Sunil was pulling funny faces and Jasmin burst into a fresh set of giggles.

"Get out." Bindra pronounced her words slowly and softly, but everybody heard.

"I'm sorry Ma'am... I... I..." Jasmin stuttered, the colour

draining from her face. Belatedly, Sunil realised his own mistake and tried to intervene.

"Ma'am, it was me. I was making her laugh. I'm sorry."

"In that case, it's even better if she is not a part of this show. Maybe you will concentrate on your steps then, huh?"

She turned around and gave Jasmin a vicious look.

"Out!"

Jasmin fled, tears streaming down her face. The rest of us stood dumbfounded. Bindra had struck again.

WE FOUND HER HIDING BEHIND THE *PEEPAL* [20]TREE. HER face was swollen and she turned her back to us as we approached her.

"Jas, I'm sorry!" Sunil was contrite, fully aware of how much she had wanted to be a part of the dance-drama. I stood silently by his side. I would've happily swapped places with her, except for the fact that Bindra wouldn't allow it and Jasmin probably wouldn't want the bit part I had.

"I hate her!" She spat out with such venom that I actually took a step back.

"She's evil," Sunil agreed, "but powerful. We need to beat her at her own game."

"How?" I asked.

"Leave it to me. I know what to do. Jas, cheer up. You don't need to be a part of this. Go join Bhalla's elocution team. You speak so well, he'll be happy to have you."

"Really?" She cheered up instantly. I could see that Sunil knew just how to pull her out of a funk. I just hugged her, which somehow turned into a group hug. Standing together, holding each other - I was suddenly overcome by a certainty that all would be well.

. . .

Vandana's face broke into a smile when she saw me at her door.

"You came!" She seemed astonished that I had kept my word. Had I really been that difficult, that unapproachable, over the last few years?

Sujata aunty came towards me and enveloped me in a hug. There was a warmth and familiarity in her embrace. A reminder of days spent in the company of people who had loved me for me, never compared me to my beautiful sister, and who, perhaps, still cared. Why had I been so suspicious of everyone's motives? So eager to shut myself off?

We ate *gujias,* chatted about school, talked about the latest movies and listened to the radio, just like old times. Aunty would walk in now and again to ask if we wanted any more snacks. It was a pleasant afternoon, and for a while I forgot that we were blighted in any way.

"Bring Meera with you the next time," Sujata aunty said as I was leaving.

I stopped and looked at her. Ma and she had fallen out years ago over Yamini Sahni. Their friendship had soured when aunty had pointed out that Ma was behaving like a hanger-on.

"She won't come."

"Then tell her I asked after her."

I walked home, wondering at the nature of our relationships with people around us after our tragedy. Had we ascribed only negative intentions to everyone, when perhaps, there had been people who had reached out to us, had been willing to help, even? Had we, in our pain, assumed only the worst in others?

Ma and aunty had been fast friends for years before Yamini Sahni entered the locality. They had had similar tastes, similar backgrounds and enjoyed each other's company immensely. Our families had been intertwined for years. Sadly, in her adoration of Yamini Sahni, Ma sacrificed a good, solid friendship with Sujata aunty. If only Ma could have differentiated between the two women, if only she could have seen the depth of one and the shallowness of the other. As it was, the consequences of her choice had been catastrophic beyond belief.

IN OUR THREE CORNERS OF THE CLASSROOM, JASMIN, SUNIL and I were not thriving. It wasn't like we didn't have any other friends, but we missed our easy camaraderie, the ability to find the same things funny; our silent kinship.

As *Chhipkali* wrote more formulae on the blackboard, my eye caught Jasmin's and she grimaced. Although somewhat recovered from her ouster from the dance-drama, she still hadn't come to terms with the fact that Sunil and I were a part of something and she wasn't. Alongside this was her distaste for all Sciences – she was a Humanities student through and through, and found these classes to be pure torture. It sufficed to say that Jasmin was not a happy girl.

There was a knock on the door, and a year 8 student peered in.

"What?" *Chhipkali* growled at her.

"Bindra ma'am wants Sunil Kashyap for rehearsals."

"No."

"But... but ma'am... she told me to bring him..."

"Tell Bindra ma'am, Sunil is studying for his pre Boards and he cannot come."

I glanced over at Sunil and noted the colour rising in his cheeks. Jasmin's mouth had fallen open. I noticed the same look replicated on most of my classmates' faces. No one stood up to Bindra. Didn't *Chhipkali* know?

Ten minutes later Bindra was standing at the door, glowering at *Chhipkali*.

"Chetna, I need Sunil for rehearsals."

"And Binny, I need him in the class. Your dance is secondary to the Board exams. You can have him once the class is finished."

"I don't think you understand. The Home Minister is our chief guest this time. The dance has to be flawless. Mrs Padhi has allowed extra rehearsals."

"Not on my time, she hasn't."

We were riveted by the exchange. No one had guessed that *Chhipkali* had the guts to stand up to Bindra. The angrier Bindra got, the more sanctimonious *Chhipkali* became. Between her darting tongue and Bindra's bulbous eyes, this drama was far more interesting than the one being presented to the Home Minister.

Suddenly they realised that they had an audience, and in tacit accord, moved outside the classroom.

"So, what happened?" Ma asked that afternoon, as I repeated the scene to her.

"Bindra won, of course! Mrs Padhi is petrified of her, and wants to make a good impression on the Minister, so *Chhipkali* had to retreat."

"Don't call your teacher that! Give her some respect. So, Sunil will be missing his lessons? That's not good."

"And he isn't happy, even though Chemistry's not his favourite subject. He's vowed for the umpteenth time to get even with Bindra. I don't know how though, because that woman can bend iron to her will."

Ma seemed distracted as she stirred the *daal* [21] in the pot. I had been hanging around the kitchen while she cooked.

Ma had taken such pride in her kitchen before. The copper pots that hung on the wall had once gleamed, polished and shiny, her tin of *masalas* [22] had been promptly refilled every day, the toaster brought by *Mausi*[23] from Kuwait had taken pride of place on the shelf, displayed as a badge of our foreign connections. Today, however, everything looked grimy and a bit tired, as though sadness had crept in and taken residence here as well.

"I went to see Lakshmi today. Took her some old clothes, a few rations and that idol I'd promised her ."

"Was she okay?"

"Puja, she's showing quite a bit now. I think it's only a matter of months."

"What?! She's only just told us..."

"That doesn't mean anything. I don't think she has much sense of time. Anyway, Mehta and her army have been to see her too."

"And?"

"I saw some new pots and pans they've donated to her and she was in a different *salwar kameez*."

"Why do you look so worried?"

"Only because something doesn't feel right. Mrs Mehta has never been magnanimous without an agenda. I can't believe she hasn't kicked up a fuss about a pregnant sweeper woman."

"Maybe Papa's little chat with Mr Mehta did the trick?"

"Hmmm," she looked unconvinced. "There is also the issue of paternity."

"Ma, she could've been pregnant before she got here. Especially if she's a lot further gone than we thought. Does it matter who the father is?"

"I suppose not. I guess I'm just worrying unnecessarily..."

"Of course you are!" I went over and hugged my mother. It had been a long time since I'd seen her so engaged in another person's life. It felt good.

. . .

SUNIL'S IMPROVEMENT IN DANCE COULD HAVE BEEN PUT down to various factors: his fear of Bindra, his reluctance to miss more classes for rehearsals, or his need to get the whole thing over and done with, with minimal fuss. At any rate, he was sticking to the cues and not resembling a bull in a china shop anymore.

No one was more pleased than Bindra. Once again, by sheer force of will and temperament, she had managed to get what she wanted. I didn't dislike her, but I was curious about people like her. People who brushed off opposition and impediments like fluff off their clothes. We were a family of thinkers, and we evaluated our words, our actions and our choices incessantly. How I wish I had the thick skin and the pushiness that Bindra possessed.

Priya Majumdar, two years our senior and extremely pretty, had taken Sunil under her wing. With sinuous grace she guided him through the steps. With a 'come hither' look, she flirted her way through the rehearsals.

"She makes me look good," Sunil explained to an increasingly petulant Jasmin. "If she wants to flirt, let her. *I'm* not falling for her."

"Everyone is talking about it! They are saying you two are a couple."

"Don't be silly Jas, I'm not going to date a girl two years older. She's nearly as old as my sister! In any case, I don't find her that pretty." Sunil always knew how to mollify Jasmin. Maybe there had always been a rapport between them, an unseen, unspoken understanding, just waiting to solidify into something more concrete. Something I could never be a part of.

VANDANA AND I DECIDED TO CHECK IN ON LAKSHMI AS WE walked home from the bus stop. We hadn't seen her around for a few days, and even though the WomSoc seemed to be helping out, we felt responsible for her.

"It's like that old Chinese proverb - 'If you save a life, you are responsible for that life'," I said to Vandy as we walked together. Not that we had saved Lakshmi's life, technically .

"Where do you learn this stuff Puja? Honestly, you are way too brainy for your own good!" She was laughing as she said this. An ease and comfort had crept back into our exchanges slowly. We never spoke of *didi*, and as long as we avoided that subject, I was happy to once again have a friendship with her.

"Who do you think the father is? Could it be one of the servants or *chowkidars*[24]? I mean, the way she reacts to men, it seems she has had some sort of horrible experience with them."

"I wouldn't ask her that, Vandy. Anyway, she keeps saying God has given her this baby, which, I suppose, in a way, He has."

"Do you think they'll take the baby away straight after it's born or a little bit later?"

I stopped and stared at her.

"What do you mean?"

"Don't you know? Mr Mehta said there's no way they'll let a mad woman and her mongrel run around our streets forever. Once the elections are over, they'll both be gone. At least, that's what he was saying to daddy..." She trailed off, noting the expression on my face.

I marched ahead of her, my thoughts in turmoil. Of course, we should have anticipated this! The Mehtas were way too wily and had only their own political ambitions in sight. Lakshmi's fate mattered little to them. Basic humanity had bypassed them a long time ago.

Lakshmi was lying on the floor groaning when we walked in.

"Kya hua?[25]" I asked, concerned that she was ill or that the baby was arriving early.

She curled herself into a ball, still shaking and whimpering.

"Puja, look!" Vandy pointed out the bruises on Laksmi's back. She had been beaten up by someone and I wanted to know who. Would Lakshmi tell us?

---

1. Tea
2. Playing cards
3. An Indian sweet made from milk solids and sugar and typically flavoured with cardamom or nuts
4. An ornamental wristband given during the Indian festival of Raksha Bandhan as an amulet or token of respect and affection, typically by a woman or girl to her brother or a man that she regards as a brother
5. A popular annual festival during which a girl or woman gives a cotton bracelet (raakhi) to a brother or someone she considers as one, who in turn treats her as a sister
6. Saree seller
7. Maid servant/Cleaner
8. Thank you
9. The other girl?
10. Are you okay?
11. Yes
12. I'm pregnant
13. Can we come inside?
14. Who is the father?
15. The baby is God's
16. No, no. I will not go there.
17. Temple
18. You are very beautiful
19. Let no evil eye fall upon her
20. Fig tree of India noted for great size and longevity
21. Lentil curry
22. Spices
23. Mother's sister
24. A watchman or gatekeeper
25. What's happened?

III

The doctor had given Lakshmi a sedative and she lay fast asleep as Ma, Vandy, Sujata aunty and I stood huddled together in the little hut.

"Is she going to be okay?" Aunty asked the doctor.

"Yes, she's fine. Luckily, she managed to protect her stomach and the baby is okay too..." He looked at us, confirming what we had feared. "Whoever did this to her wanted her to lose the baby."

Once the doctor had left, we stood around in the little hut for a while and then on a mutual consensus stepped outside, letting Lakshmi sleep peacefully.

"Meera, this is very worrying." Aunty looked my mother in the face as she mouthed these words. Up until now they had studiously avoided addressing each other directly. An unease from their long feud still lingered.

"Yes, I know." Ma looked towards Vandy and me, then took Aunty's elbow and walked to one side, speaking softly.

I looked at Vandy and she looked back at me, the same shock and horror I was feeling writ large on her face.

"Who would want to harm poor Lakshmi?"

"Probably the same person who impregnated her."

We hadn't been able to extract any information from Lakshmi, despite trying to cajole her into revealing who had done this to her.

"Such monsters exist in this world..."

"And look at our mothers trying to shield us from reality. As if we aren't able to see or hear or process things for ourselves."

"That's because they love us Puja. Or, maybe they do know more than us?"

She glanced back at the hut and I said what she was thinking. "She will have to be moved out of here. She isn't safe. Not if someone wants her to lose the baby."

Vandy nodded in agreement. "Maybe she'll tell us who it is?"

"I hope so, but somehow, I think she's too scared to..."

VANDY AND I WERE EXCLUDED FROM THE CONCLAVE. MA and Papa and Vandy's parents sat in the living room, talking about Lakshmi's situation, while the two of us who had brought it to their attention to begin with, hovered outside.

"Puja, forget it! The adults will be better at sorting things out. What can you and I do anyway? No point getting annoyed about it."

"Vandy, all along I have seen adults make a mess of things. What makes you think this time will be any different?"

She looked at me, this little girl I had known nearly all my life, this little girl who was now a prepossessing teenager, her eyes brimming with all the innocence and belief in her parents' wisdom. Belief I had once harboured myself, before life had taught me differently. She looked at me and simply said, "Puja, when will you forgive?"

My breath caught in my throat.

Forgive? Forgive whom, I wanted to scream! Forgive my parents for their ignorance, forgive the world for mocking and whispering, forgive myself for being helpless, or forgive my sister for leaving?

I turned away. It was all I could do not to punch Vandy in the face. My anger, I knew, was disproportionate to this particular situation, but it bubbled inside me constantly, threatening to erupt and destroy everything in its path. My anger and my grief were like twin clamps that squeezed and squeezed till I felt breathless with fatigue and pain.

I walked into the living room as I heard Papa say, "I've spoken to my contact at the women's shelter. She is willing to take Lakshmi in for the duration of her pregnancy, but she will have to be rehoused later. As it is, they are short of beds and funds. We will have to make some sort of monetary donation."

"Anuj, you saw how agitated she got when we suggested this the last time. I don't think she'll agree."

"She has no choice... What's worse? Staying here with the threat to her life, or moving to safer surroundings, even if she doesn't like them?"

"Why can't we keep her?"

Four sets of eyes turned to stare at me.

"We have a spare room attached to the garage. Why can't we keep her there?"

"Don't be ridiculous, Puja. We can't take responsibility for her, especially in her condition... Besides, how will it look to the rest of the locality? They'll think... they'll think... Papa was responsible for her state."

I could feel my face turning hot as the words spewed out of me. "Why has it always been about other people? Let them think what they want! Were 'they' around when *didi* died? Did they care then? If you and Papa hadn't been so bothered about other people's opinions, maybe she would have been alive today!"

I saw the shocked look on their faces, and turned and ran out of the room.

WE DIDN'T SPEAK TO ONE ANOTHER FOR A FEW DAYS AFTER that. Not sure what decision they'd arrived at, I had locked myself in my room, unwilling and unable to participate in poor Lakshmi's fate being decided by strangers to her.

I had always been prone to retreat within myself, even when *didi* had been alive. It was my way of coming to terms with things that were outside of my control. At times like these, books were my refuge. I studied, read and researched, and spoke very little.

Ma and Papa, thankfully, were used to this. They left me to it. *Didi* had been the only one who would try and needle me out of my black moods. She used to say that I was letting things fester, that communication was the only way forward, that I needed to talk about my problems before I could arrive at a resolution. Oh, the irony!

I had tried, in the last few years, to snap myself out of this habit. More for the sake of Ma and Papa. After *didi,* they had no one, save me. I tried to become a pale facsimile of their ideal daughter, the one they had lost.

Yet, right now, I felt they deserved nothing but my aloofness and my disgust. They were not particularly happy with my outburst either. So, we avoided each other, silence once again shrouding our household as it had done for two years.

School was no better. Jasmin and Sunil were fighting once again, and between their lovers' tiffs, the additional work being assigned in preparation for the mock exams and the dance rehearsals, I felt increasingly isolated.

There were days when I wondered if there was any point

in carrying on. Whether there had been some gigantic cosmic mistake where the wrong sister had been taken accidentally. Whether my miserable existence was my punishment for still being alive.

Vandana and I had also gone back to our usual routine after school. Either she would walk ahead of me or I would, each one pretending to be in a hurry, avoiding each other's eyes and company.

Maybe my outburst had stalled the tentative coming together of our families. To me, it once again demonstrated the callowness of the people around us. In the good and happy times, we had been surrounded by friends and family, only to be abandoned when disaster struck. We were the pariahs of the locality, the ones people side-stepped for fear of being contaminated by our bad luck.

I HADN'T SEEN LAKSHMI IN A WHILE AND DECIDED TO knock on her rickety door. She took a while getting to it. When she saw it was me, she beamed and led me inside. I noticed little bundles, all wrapped up, sitting around the hut.

"Yeh kya hai? Aap kahin ja rahe ho?"[1]

Even as I asked her where she was going, there was a sinking feeling in the pit of my stomach. They must have convinced her to move. What lies had they fed her? What pressure had they used to coerce her? What would become of this poor woman and her baby?

"Aapke ghar hi toh aa rahi hoon. Aapki mataji ne bulaya hai."[2]

I stood rooted to the spot, my thoughts in tumult. In all my anger and resentment against my parents, had I forgotten that they were ultimately good and kind souls? When had they changed their minds and decided to house Lakshmi? Why hadn't they told me?

I reached forward and hugged Lakshmi, ignoring her

45

stale, unwashed odour. She stood still in my embrace, neither fighting nor succumbing to it. I held her and wept, for the first time in a long time.

NOTHING WAS SAID AT HOME. NOTHING NEEDED ANY saying. Almost organically, we fell back into our natural rhythms, the air having been cleared of all negativity. Ma seemed happy to have Lakshmi around, and although Papa wasn't altogether comfortable with the arrangement, he could see that we were pleased, and that pleased him.

Lakshmi had grown quite rotund in her pregnancy, and even though she was still officially employed by the NA to sweep the streets, her living conditions were so much improved that she seemed to be a new person entirely. Ma showered her with old *salwar kameezes* and *saris*. She even gave her an old perfume bottle of *didi*'s that none of us had had the heart to throw away.

Washed, clean, well nourished and well looked after, Lakshmi positively blossomed. Her quarters were small but neatly kept. She had a proper bed with proper bedding. She had curtains, a small table and chair, a compact attached bath and toilet, and most importantly, she had a door she could lock from the inside. Even though her little room was attached to the garage, we would still hear anyone trying to break in or attack her. The arrangement seemed perfectly adequate.

Ma was packing my lunch as she said, "Puja, maybe this is God's way of letting us make amends..."

I looked down at my hands. I guess each one of us had to believe in something to make ourselves feel better.

"YOU WERE MAKING EYES AT HER!"

"Don't be ridiculous! I'm supposed to be in love with her. What am I to do - glare at her?"

Priya was, once again, the topic of the day. I dipped in and out of their argument, preferring to read my book instead. It was lunch time and we were sitting together under the *peepal*[3] tree. It had barely taken five minutes for Jasmin to launch into her latest grievance. I could tell that Sunil was finding it tiresome now, but I also wondered if he wasn't deliberately provoking her as well. I had seen the way he looked at Priya, and privately sympathised with Jasmin's jealousy. Nonetheless, I refused to get involved, no matter how hard Jasmin tried.

"You were there, Puja! Tell me, wasn't he fawning all over that horrid creature?"

"He was acting, Jasmin. He was copying whatever Bindra wanted him to do."

"Oh yes! Bindra is suddenly his favourite teacher too. What happened to 'I'll show her', 'I'll teach her a lesson' etc etc?"

Sunil frowned at her and then stood up and walked away. Jasmin started to cry softly.

"Hey, hey, don't cry... He's just annoyed. He'll be back soon enough."

"Puja, he called me a drama queen. He said that I was overreacting and that I needed to get a life!"

Jasmin had always been self-absorbed, but because she was essentially a kind and sunny person, it was easy to overlook this flaw. Lately though, her prickliness had highlighted the fact that to her, the world revolved around her little person. No one else was allowed to have thoughts or emotions, if she weren't a part of them. Maybe it was an only-child syndrome, but I was slowly losing patience with this self-absorption.

"And how are you Puja? What's been happening in your life? Are you happy? Are you well?" The words came out unbidden, from some deep, resentful place that I had been quashing for way too long. I knew I sounded snarky and irritable, but that's how I felt, and it was time Jasmin realised that we weren't just supporting actors to the 'Jasmin Show'.

She looked up at me, astonished. Her face was pink, the tears still running down her cheeks. I looked at her pretty face, sighed loudly, picked up my book and lunchbox and walked away in the opposite direction to Sunil.

THEY WERE ALL SITTING THERE, LIKE VULTURES READY TO pick at a carcass. My mother sat between them, looking cowed. It was evident they had been there a while from the half-empty teacups that littered the table. Mrs Mehta was mid-rant when I nearly walked into the living room, stopping short at the door.

"I cannot believe you'd take her in without consulting the WomSoc. You don't even know whose bastard she's carrying. Meera, I would have thought you'd have more sense after what happened to your own daughter, but clearly not..."

Sujata aunty stood up.

"Mrs Mehta, there is no need to drag that issue into this. I'm sure they had nothing but the best of intentions when they brought Lakshmi in."

I watched quietly from the doorway. No one had noticed me yet.

"What intentions? Were we not taking care of her? She had everything she needed. We would have provided her with medical care as well, when the time came. Not like she'd deliver the baby on the street."

Mrs Mehta's blouse was soaked with sweat, and her double chin trembled as she spoke, a bead hanging off it. For a do-gooder, she had an incredibly bad temperament. Her frown lines and the wrinkles around her mouth were testament to a lifetime of foul moods and temper tantrums. We'd often wondered in the privacy of our home whether the reason she managed to continue as the chairperson of so many committees was because most people were too afraid to cross her.

My mother, never the most assertive person, was practically cowering under the onslaught. The other women wittered on, led easily like sheep by Mrs Mehta.

"I'm simply saying that there was no need to bring that woman into their house. She is an employee of the Municipality and paid by them. So why is she living here?"

"Because, as I told you before, she was attacked. Her life and probably the baby's too, is in danger." Sujata aunty looked annoyed.

"Pffft! Such nonsense. Must have been some client knocking her about. Who knows what she gets up to in her spare time?"

I couldn't take it any longer.

"Mrs Mehta, I think it's time you left."

They all turned to stare at me.

"What did you say Puja?"

"I said, it's time you left. And I'll tell you why as well. None of you ladies have any business coming into our house and telling us what to do. We don't need your 'advice' or your 'help'."

Sujata aunty came over to me and put her hand on my shoulder.

"Puja, I'm sorry. This is my fault. I thought we could do something for Lakshmi as a community, rather than letting it all fall to you." She glanced over at the glowering Mrs Mehta. "I should have known better."

One by one, the women stood up and started to file out. Mrs Mehta glared at me and then at looked at my mother, clearly enunciating her oncoming salvo.

"Meera, I'd watch out. This one will go the same way as your first."

I slammed the door hard behind her retreating back, then turned and hugged my weeping mother.

THE ANNUAL DAY PRODUCTION WAS GOING TO BE ON THE 14th of November, *Chacha* [4]Nehru's birthday. Why we call a deceased Prime Minister of the country our uncle, I've never understood, but his birthday was celebrated in all schools as a mark of respect and recognition of his love for children.

The frequency of the rehearsals had increased considerably, and it seemed as though the teachers were resigned to their students being hijacked willy-nilly out of classes. Bindra was in her element, lording it over everyone, making sure the stage design was exactly to her vision. Mr Bose, the art teacher, was run ragged trying to keep up with the frequent changes in her vision.

The chemistry between Sunil and Priya was evident to all, and word had once again gotten back to Jasmin. This time, however, she had resorted to giving him the cold shoulder. After my little sally at her, I had been consigned to Siberia as well. Sunil had tried complaining about Jasmin to me, but I was so fed up with their petty dramas that I had just walked away. Our tiny little group had splintered and we were left to our own devices.

As a back-up dancer, I had a lot of sitting around to do. Several girls used this time to talk about their crushes, sneaking peeks at the handsome older boys as they played hockey on the field. I used it to study. People knew not to mock or disturb me; I was so cantankerous these days that everyone gave me a wide berth.

It was also the time when I started to wonder if my future really lay in India. For all our traditions and values, I felt that as a society, we were controlling, stifling, conservative and regressive. There had been a time I could never have envisioned leaving my country or my family. Now, it seemed like the best way forward.

I knew that my parents could ill afford to send me abroad. The only way I could manage it was through studying hard enough to get into a premier university, through which I'd be able to apply for a scholarship overseas. The path ahead was becoming clearer by the day, and if it meant I'd have to work my socks off, I was more than willing to do so.

AS I WALKED PAST LAKSHMI'S HUT, HER FORMER ABODE, I once again wondered about her antecedents. Where was she from, where was her family, how had she ended up in our locality and who had attacked her the other night? Was Lakshmi even safe with us? How long would my parents withstand the pressure? What we'd do once the baby came was another question altogether.

Ma and she were shelling peas on the balcony. The radio was blaring inside, and I had to laugh at them nodding along to whatever nonsensical song they were humming. They seemed to be in such perfect harmony, two kindred souls working together, each lost in their own thoughts, but pleased to have the other's company, that momentarily I forgot all my concerns.

Lakshmi looked up and smiled.

"*Chai peeyogi*[5]?"

I nodded and she quickly brushed down her *kurta* [6]and bustled into the kitchen to make me a cup of tea.

"What are you making for dinner Ma?"

"*Baingan bhurta* [7]and *aloo muttar*[8]," Ma carried on shelling peas, "Lakshmi is such a help, Puja. She insisted on washing all the sheets today, and is talking about taking down the curtains tomorrow. So much energy... I keep telling her to take it easy in her condition, but she doesn't stop..."

"It's good *na* Ma? As long as the doctor thinks she's okay, let her do it. She probably just wants to show her gratitude."

Ma nodded, then looked up at me.

"She came across Ambika's picture today and asked me about her."

"W...what did you say?"

"I told her it was my elder daughter and that she'd gone away."

"Gone away?"

"What could I say Puja? I didn't want to tell her what happened..."

'Gone away' implied that at some point the person might return. 'Gone away' implied choice, motivation and destination. None of this applied to *didi*'s departure from our lives.

"Why didn't you just say she died? When are we going to confront the truth about what happened?"

"Oh Puja!"

PERHAPS WE SHOULD HAVE GUESSED SOMETHING WAS AMISS when *didi* became secretive. When she'd want to use the phone at odd hours and look devastated when the conversation didn't last more than a few minutes. Or maybe when she heard that Rajat's visa to the US had come through and he would be leaving for an indefinitely long time, and she locked herself in her room. Or maybe even when she started to hide her widened girth beneath voluminous clothes, her face pale, drawn and worried.

But sometimes it's easy to overlook that which is staring you right in the face. After all, each of us wants the truth to conform to our version of reality. For Ma and Papa, *didi* was the impeccable daughter: studious, talented, polite and beautiful. For me, she was the ideal I struggled to live up to. None of us bothered to see what else there might have been beyond that perfect facade.

Who knows which back alley she went to? Which quack performed a botched abortion on her? Where she got the money to pay him? Did we even wonder why she came home late in an auto rickshaw, citing some lame excuse? Were we so ignorant, so insensitive that we didn't pick up on her distress or her desperation?

All we saw was the blood and life ebbing out of her. All we heard was her plaintive cry in the middle of the night, and the sight of the blood-soaked sheets as she haemorrhaged. Papa's frantic 100 call for an ambulance, Ma cradling her child, crying and whispering her prayers, my stupefied horror at watching *didi's* tenuous grasp on life loosen with every shallow breath.

Nothing prepares you for death - the finality of it, the heartbreak that follows, the questions that haunt you, the 'maybes', the 'what ifs'. It took months to piece together the sequence of events. Her romance with Rajat, their assignations, the secrets they'd kept, his betrayal and her desperation...

Ma had insisted on confronting the Sahnis. Yamini Sahni had been vicious in her denouncement of *didi*. Ma had sobbed recounting the words: gold digger, opportunist, whore. Ambika *didi*, my kind, gentle, beautiful sister had been reduced to an ugly smear.

The Sahnis rented out their house and moved to Gurgaon. Rajat left for America. And we were left adrift in an ocean of pain.

---

1. What's all this? Are you going somewhere?
2. I'm coming to your house. Your mother has invited me to stay.
3. Fig tree

4. Uncle/ Father's brother
5. Will you have some tea?
6. Loose top
7. Mashed aubergine/eggplant
8. Potatoes and peas curry

IV

Lakshmi went into labour at 3 a.m. Ma shook me awake from my slumber.

"We are taking her to the nursing home now. I just didn't want you to wake up and worry."

I worried regardless. They were gone all night, and in the morning as I left for school, I wondered when they would be back.

It was the day of dress rehearsals and the entire cast and crew of the production had gathered in the hall. Well ahead of the schedule, Bindra wanted at least a month for the costumes to be fitted or altered as per requirement. Now, costumes of all shapes, sizes and materials were piled together with the teachers calling out names and assigning them to the various cast members. Priya was floating around in a diaphanous red number, clearly the star and acting it too. Sunil was trying out various *kurtas*[1] and finding them all too short.

Someone came up behind me and whispered, "Boo!" I turned around, startled, only to see Jasmin standing there grinning ear to ear.

"What are you doing here?"

"I'm helping with the set design. I asked Mr Bose if I could join the team."

"But you can't even draw a straight line..."

"So what? I can use a paint brush. All I have to do is paint the trees and bushes in the background."

"You're really here to keep an eye on Sunil, aren't you?"

She blushed. "I'm sorry you've had to go through all this drama with us Puja, and I'm sorry I've been so inconsiderate. I'm just lonely without the two of you. I'm here to be close to you both, and if you don't want me here, I'll go away."

I looked at her miserable face and burst out laughing.

"Don't be silly! Of course, I'm happy to have you here... and so is Sunil. Look at him."

Sunil was wearing a parrot green *kurta* and waving wildly at us.

"I think he's happy something's finally fit him," She noted wryly. We burst into giggles, and I felt like life was back on track again.

I didn't want to say anything about Lakshmi's labour to them. Just for a while, I wanted to keep my two worlds separate from each other.

I RUSHED HOME FROM THE BUS STOP, PASSING BY VANDY with a quick wave. All day I'd been thinking about Lakshmi and her baby. I'd been hoping and praying that all had gone well and that the baby was healthy.

Ma stood at the doorway, a big smile on her face.

"It's a boy."

All of the day's pent-up anxiety was released in my relieved gasp.

"Can I see them?"

"Not yet. She's asleep. It wasn't an easy labour, and the baby is a little underweight."

"Is he okay? And Lakshmi?"

"They are both fine, just exhausted. It isn't called labour for nothing."

"Where's Papa?"

"He's gone to buy some *ladoos*[2] from the *Halwai*[3]."

I shook off my satchel and sat down as Ma started to organise my lunch. Already the air seemed lighter, as though this brand new soul had somehow lifted the heaviness of grief off our home.

"Ma?"

"Yes Puja?"

"What's she calling the baby?"

"Krishna. She's never changed her mind about that."

"No, I mean the surname. What will his surname be?"

Ma came out of the kitchen, the *belan*[4] still in her hand, her brow furrowed in thought.

"I honestly don't know..."

KRISHNA WAS A BEAUTIFUL BABY. HE WAS CHARCOAL BLACK, and had inherited his mother's unusual eyes - one grey and one brown.

"They could change colour, you know," Sujata aunty declared, as she held him in her arms. Aside from our family, only Vandy and Sujata aunty were allowed to hold him. Lakshmi was watchful and protective, as though sensing the intentions of Mehta and company.

In the three weeks since Krishna's birth, Mrs Mehta had made overtures towards Ma to come and see the baby. Each one had been rebuffed at the behest of Pa and I. We had convinced Ma not to let Mrs Mehta and her coterie in until we arrived at a suitable solution. The local elections were only a few weeks away, and Mrs Mehta was undoubtedly trying to use the situation to her advantage.

Now Pa walked in, holding a letter. He looked annoyed and indicated that we follow him outside. Sujata aunty gently handed Krishna back to Lakshmi.

"I've just received a threatening letter from the Municipality." He showed us the letter. "They are accusing Lakshmi of dereliction of duty, and us of housing her without permission. If she doesn't show up to work in the next five days, she will be fired and we will be fined."

Ma gasped, "Can they do that?!"

"I suspect this is Mehta pulling strings. And yes, they can fire her, but I'm not so sure that they can impose a fine on us. This is just some bombastic nonsense to try and frighten us."

"What are you going to do Papa?"

"I'll tell you what I'm going to do. I'm going to stand against the idiot in the elections. If he thinks he can try these stunts on me, he's got another think coming."

"Anuj, is that wise?" Sujata aunty looked worried. "He's a very well-connected man, and has been campaigning for months in advance. You won't stand a chance."

"I'm not doing it to win, Sujata, I just want to dilute his voter base. The more divided their sympathies, the less likely *he* is to win."

I looked at all their worried faces and sighed inwardly. Were we unwittingly stirring a hornets' nest?

REHEARSALS WERE RATCHETING UP AS NOVEMBER approached. Everybody had given up the pretence of study. Those involved in the dance-drama were busy practising their cues, those on the periphery were enjoying the down time and those completely uninvolved were revelling in the unexpected break. Even some of the teachers had been roped in to help, and were heard complaining to one another about Bindra's bossy ways.

Sunil, Jasmin and I were reunited and once again happy to spend time with each other. Our little separation had made us see the error of our ways. Sunil had stopped paying attention to Priya, Jasmin had dropped the self-pity and I had become a little less cranky.

"So Papa has decided to stand against Mr Mehta in the local elections. Funnily enough, so many people have come out in his support that there is a very real chance that he may even win!"

"Good for uncle!" Sunil stated this with relish. He was always in support of the underdog, and Papa's stance had stirred all of Sunil's protective instincts towards Lakshmi and our family.

"Do you think that your taking Lakshmi in might be working in uncle's favour?" Jasmin said slowly. "I mean, didn't the Mehtas want to use the same kinda thing for themselves? Only, you guys did it out of genuine concern. People can sense that, you know."

We had been pleasantly surprised by the number of people who had dropped in, phoned or simply accosted Papa on the street to say they would vote for him. Sujata aunty had been vociferous in her support, and although the Municipality had indeed fired Lakshmi, no further threatening letters had come our way.

"What are you going to do with the mad sweeper woman, though?"

"She's not mad Jasmin, just a tiny bit eccentric. She still does a few crazy things from time to time, but nothing that will harm anyone, least of all us or her baby. Papa has been thinking of relocating her to our house in Darjeeling so she can live there as our caretaker. We know some people there who can watch out for her. We are certain that Krishna and she will be safe in that environment."

Papa's idea had surprised us, but Ma and I had readily agreed. No one knew where our little cottage was, and Lakshmi had already demonstrated that she was adept at keeping house. It seemed to be the ideal solution.

"Come on, come on! Less chitter chatter. Get up! Sunil, you need to go over the *Vrindavan*⁵ dance again. Priya, come here..."

With a sigh and an eye roll, Sunil got up and joined the troupe on stage. Jasmin looked at me and said, "Don't worry Puja, everything will work out."

At a little over a month old, Krishna was carried on Lakshmi's back in a baby sling we had fashioned from an old *dupatta*⁶ of Ma's. She wanted to get back on her feet, but was scared to leave Krishna alone for even a moment.

He was a placid baby, seldom upset, and happy to be near his mother. Soon, we became accustomed to seeing mother and baby together, as Lakshmi busied herself with chores around the house.

She would often hum songs to him, not always *filmi*⁷ ones. One day, out of curiosity, I asked her, "*Aap kahaan se ho*⁸?"

"Orissa," she answered absently as she rinsed the pans in the sink.

Sensing an opening I pushed on. "*Aapke mata-pita*⁹?"

"*Wahin pe hain. Mujhko nikaal diya.*¹⁰"

"*Lekin kyun*¹¹?"

"*Vidhwa hoon, tabhi*¹²."

"Oh."

Lakshmi had been expelled from her home for being a widow. I felt even more keenly for this young woman who stated her truth in such a matter-of-fact manner. How many years of neglect, sadness and exploitation lay behind those words?

As a young widow, what must she have gone through once abandoned by her own parents? How many had used and abused her? It was no wonder that her grip on reality was fragile at best.

I watched her wash the dishes, rocking Krishna on her back and my eyes filled with tears. How inward-looking I'd been in the last few years, focussing only on my pain and loss, when all around me there were people whose wounds were just as deep, whose lives were just as, if not more, harrowing.

MRS MEHTA LANDED UP A MONTH AFTER KRISHNA'S BIRTH. It was early November and the days were turning chilly. She had a little package in her hand, wrapped in a big bow. A peace offering, we surmised. It turned out to be a little blue sweater she had knit herself. This surprised us.

Lakshmi shrank back as she offered the gift to her. Ma hovered watchfully, waiting for the real Mrs Mehta to emerge from behind this kind, gift-bearing stranger. It was I who brought her a cup of *chai*[13] and chocolate biscuits.

"Thank you Puja! *Arre dekho toh sahi... maine apne haathon se banaaya hai...*[14]" When Lakshmi still refused to accept the package, Mrs Mehta tore open the wrapping to reveal the pale blue sweater within. Despite herself, Lakshmi's eyes lit up and she reached forward tentatively to take it from her.

"I am sorry for my harsh words Meera. I am not myself these days." Her lips quivered as she looked at Ma. "I realise that I was too quick to judge..." She stole a glance at Lakshmi, "Too quick to condemn..."

Ma looked at her askance. In all the years we had lived in this locality, Mrs Mehta had never displayed an ounce of humility.

"What brings you here Mrs Mehta? If this is to ask Anuj to withdraw his nomination, then I'm sorry, it's out of my hands. Men will do what they want to."

"Don't I just know it? No Meera, that was not my intention at all. In fact, I have a proposition for you. I'd like you to join me as Vice President of the WomSoc. I'm getting older, and I need someone I can trust, someone who has already displayed her altruistic disposition. Who better than you?"

I sat next to Lakshmi, playing with Krishna's toes as he gurgled, but my every sense was on alert, waiting to hear what Ma said in response.

"T... that's really kind of you, but I'll have to consult with Anuj first, before I accept your offer. I hope you understand?"

"Of course! I didn't expect an immediate answer anyway. Get back to me whenever you can. The position will remain open for you."

She stood up suddenly, leaning forward to pat Krishna's head.

"Our Lord Krishna was just as dark skinned as this little one. Mark my words, he will be a blessing to this household."

Then she turned and left, the tea and biscuits untouched.

WE WERE WALKING THROUGH A TEA PLANTATION, THE RAIN soft on our faces. A mist lingered in the air, lending an ethereal look to our surroundings. Didi kept admonishing me for plucking the tea leaves. She got crosser and crosser, frowning at me as I crushed them between my thumb and finger. Then suddenly she was Mrs Mehta, offering me a sweater too big, the knitting needles clacking together... clack, clack, clack. Her chin kept quivering as she concentrated on her knitting, the sweater growing and covering everything around her, stifling the tea plants, reaching out over the horizon till all I could see was pale blue...

I woke up sweating. That was such a vivid dream, it took me a while to shake it off. It was nearly dawn so I made myself a cup of tea and took it outside to the balcony, where Papa was already seated with his cup of coffee. He looked up and smiled as I sat myself in the wicker chair opposite him.

"*Badam*[15]?" He offered me a handful of almonds. I shook my head refusing them. He munched on them silently, taking occasional sips from his mug.

"What did you think of Mrs Mehta's proposition Papa?"

"They are clever, those two."

"How do you mean?"

"You know that old adage - 'Keep your friends close, keep your enemies closer'?"

"Yes... Oh, you mean that's what she wants to do? Give Ma a position so that she can get information out of her? But why? What could Ma possibly tell her?"

He shrugged. "I'm guessing they are feeling threatened and are willing to go to any lengths. Maybe they want us on their side so that there's no conflict of interest, or maybe they want to find a chink in my armour."

"Do you think you could win?"

"I don't know," he said this slowly, even thoughtfully, "but I was approached by a political party that said that if I won this local election, they might have bigger things in mind for me..."

"Papa, you've always said politics is a dirty game, and once you're in it you can't help but get your hands filthy. Why would you want to do that?"

"Puja, if people like us don't do anything, it allows people like the Mehtas to win."

I didn't like this, not one bit, but what could I say to my father to make him change his mind?

. . .

VANDY AND I MADE A DAY OUT OF IT, STICKING POSTERS ON walls, trees, pillars - any available surface we could find. The posters had been printed gratis for Papa by an old friend who also happened to despise the Mehtas. The trouble was that this old friend's command over the English language was not exactly the best and many of the spellings on the poster exhorting people to vote for Papa were wrong, or downright confusing.

ANUJ SHARMA FRO LOKAL COUNSELOR.

I seemed to be the only one bothered by the glaring errors.

"I think people will get the idea Puja, don't worry too much about it. Anyway look, most of the poster is uncle's face. That's what they need to focus on, right?"

Papa did look really good in the photo. This had been taken when he had a fuller face and his eyes smiled. These days the haunted look in his eyes was slowly being replaced by a quiet determination.

"I wish Papa had looked these over before giving them the go-ahead."

"You're too much of a stickler. Have you seen the Mehtas' poster? They look like they are heading out to a wedding. She's got so much gold jewellery on her, and he's wearing a *bandhgala*[16] suit. What kind of a message is that sending out? Vote for us because we're rich?"

"Why does he have Mrs Mehta on the poster? Only he is standing for the election."

"Because he wants to be perceived as the ideal family man, promoting the right values etc."

"Oh."

"Puja... I didn't want to tell you this, but I think you

should know... They are going to rehash the whole Ambika *didi* episode."

"What?!"

"Yes. Mr Ratnani was telling Papa that he overheard Mr Mehta saying that it's time 'we taught the Sharmas a lesson.'"

Politics was indeed a dirty game.

"YOU WILL COME FOR THE SHOW, RIGHT?" I LOOKED AT MY parents as they ate together. Lakshmi was making hot *chapatis*[17] in the kitchen.

"How could we miss it? What are you this time – a tree or a deer?" Papa looked at me, a wicked grin on his face.

"Anuj! Stop teasing her. It'll be nice to watch, I'm sure. Puja has been telling me how hard they've been working on it. Of course, we'll come!"

"I mean, I don't really care..." I tried to look nonchalant. "I just need a lift back..."

I remember how eagerly they'd await *didi*'s shows, how much praise they would shower on her star turns, how we would all go out for dinner afterwards to a Chinese restaurant, talking and laughing and discussing the show late into the night. I guessed that watching their second daughter melt into the background wasn't really their idea of a fun evening.

Papa looked at my face, quietly placed the piece of *chapatti* in his hand back onto his plate and came over to me.

"Puja, we would come and watch you paint a wall, if that made you happy. I was just pulling your leg." He yanked lightly at my ponytail. "Cheer up! It'll be over soon and you can get back to what you love most – sitting for exams."

We both burst out laughing. Ma looked confused, but I felt a warm glow inside of me. He did understand me, after all.

. . .

TEN DAYS TO THE SHOW AND A FORTNIGHT TO THE elections, the air seemed pregnant with anticipation. Papa's campaign had been clean, fought on fair principles and a demonstration of good faith. The Mehtas' had been a bag of dirty tricks. They had indulged in exactly the sort of mud-slinging we had been warned about.

Mrs Mehta had reverted to type, spreading rumours about our family, making out that *didi* had been a part of the oldest profession in the world, as though she had supplemented her pocket money by being a college-going call girl, had several abortions, finally dying of the one that went wrong.

"How could she? She has daughters of her own! She knew Ambika, she knew what she was like..."

Two days before the show, Ma sat weeping, horrified at the rumours and innuendos that had filtered back to her. Sujata aunty was patting her back and Lakshmi hovered nearby.

"Meera, those of us that know you, know what a pack of lies all of this is. For the rest, if they have any sense, they will realise that these are not the sort of people we want representing us."

"Ma, they are running scared. They know that Papa is in the lead, which is why they are resorting to these tactics."

"But our name is being dragged through the mud... Ambika's name!"

"Ignore them, Meera, they are not worth your time. They've shown themselves to be the petty, horrible people that they are. A lot of the locality ladies have started to leave the committee and Mrs Mehta just has her tiny little group of sycophants now. Everybody else has seen what a toxic couple they are."

Lakshmi squatted down in front of Ma and stroked her face. She took Krishna out of the sling and placed him in

Ma's lap, knowing that was a sure fire way to cheer her up. Ma looked at the sleeping baby in her arms, and smiled wanly. Lakshmi sat back on her haunches watching them closely, almost as though she was standing guard over them. Sujata aunty and I exchanged glances, heavy with a silent blend of relief and anger.

THE DAY OF THE SHOW DAWNED BRIGHT AND A LITTLE chilly. I had my costume packed neatly in my satchel, and as I went to say goodbye to my parents, a feeling of disquiet came over me. It had been an emotional and difficult week for all. For the first time in years we had sat and discussed what happened to *didi*. My own confession had not been received well.

"If you knew she was seeing that Sahni boy, why didn't you tell us, Puja?"

"She was embarrassed, Ma! How could she suddenly confess to being in love with a boy she had been tying a *rakhi*[18] to, and calling brother?"

"Had we known…" Papa had looked at me thoughtfully.

"What would you have done, Anuj? Forbidden her from seeing him? You think that would have made a difference?"

"He used and discarded her, Meera, not too different from the way that Yamini used and discarded you. Can you still not see it?"

After that, every single slight and accusation buried deep within them had come hurtling out. I'd sat in the midst of it all, feeling lost and alone.

"You are no better than Mr Mehta! All you're thinking of is your own ambition. Your family doesn't matter…"

"So, for the first time in my life, I'm trying to do something that makes a difference, and you want me to give up because you can't take the heat?"

"The heat? All I have done ALL my life is take the heat! First from your mother, and now from society. Being married to you hasn't exactly been a bed of roses, Anuj."

"Then leave! You threatened to retire to an Ashram after Ambika's death. Why don't you? There is nothing here for you. Puja and I are not worthy, are we?"

Then Ma had started to cry again, and Papa had walked out of the room, anger writ large on his face.

MA WAS NOW HELPING LAKSHMI PREPARE BREAKFAST IN THE kitchen. Krishna lay on a little mat on the floor, sucking on his toe.

"How does he do that?"

Ma looked at me and smiled, "Babies are very flexible Puja. You used to do that too."

I grabbed a *paratha*[19] from the plate and sat down at the table, watching the two women busy together. What divine providence had brought Lakshmi into our lives, I didn't know, but despite the tension in our household, at least Ma had a companion of sorts. Her own sister had moved to Kuwait many years ago, and contact with her was sporadic. Papa had been an only child, so we had very little family around us. Lakshmi and Krishna had become family now, and I was glad.

"The show starts at 7 p.m. Ma. Be there early to get seats in the front."

"Yes, I'll try. Depends on what time Papa finishes work, but I reminded him this morning."

"Has he left already?"

"Yes, he said he needed to get a few things sorted, if he was to finish early."

"Oh, okay. I'd better leave now. See you later Ma!"

I went over and gave her a little kiss on the cheek. She seemed startled as I wasn't prone to displays of affection.

Lakshmi came to the front door and smiled as she handed me my satchel.

"*Sab theek ho jayega*[20]." She patted me on my head, and I nodded, gulping at the lump in my throat.

Sunil looked rather dashing in his costume, and Jasmin kept fluttering around him. Mr Bose was annoyed as she really needed to be finishing the leaves on the tree.

"Jasmin, I think you better get back to the set," I warned her as I saw Mr Bose heading towards us. She grabbed the brush and with a quick wink at us, scuttled off before he could reach her.

"She is such an imp!" Sunil grinned at me.

"Hmmm..." My mind was elsewhere. I couldn't shake off the weird feeling I'd had all day.

"Get yourself in the make-up chair now, Kashyap!" Bindra glowered at Sunil, who had been side-stepping the make-up artist for a while now, in the hope that he could avoid being powdered, rouged and kohled like the other boys. Clearly Bindra wasn't going to have it.

Priya gave him a disdainful look as she walked past. Her red and gold costume shimmered on her slim frame, her eyes had been lined to emphasise their almond shape, her mouth painted crimson; a beauty spot on her cheek. She looked stunning, and she was well aware of the fact.

Most of the boys in our school were in love with her, so it perturbed her to no end that Sunil had withdrawn his attentions and transferred them back to Jasmin. Priya was the sort of girl who liked to receive adulation, but was loath to give it herself. Sunil's deliberate inattention was galling and she was not one to forgive a slight.

I had already been made up by one of the assistants. I was not a lead, so my make up didn't matter. I'd barely bothered to look in the mirror, knowing full well that I was not blessed in the looks department.

"YOU LOOK SO PRETTY, PUJA!" I TURNED AROUND TO SEE Vandy behind me.

"Oh, come on!"

"No, seriously. You should use *kajal*[21] more often."

I brushed off her compliment knowing that Vandy just wanted me to feel good about myself.

"Are your parents coming this evening?" I enquired.

"No, they can't be bothered. If I was in the show, they would've come. But, as I'm just assisting with the costumes, they said to get a lift home with you. Is that okay?" Vandy asked.

"Of course! Just meet me backstage after the show. We might go out for dinner afterwards, but we'll get you home by 11:30 p.m. latest."

"They won't mind as long as they know I'm with you."

"Great!"

We smiled at each other. No one would ever replace Ambika *didi* in my life, but maybe, just maybe, Vandy could become that sister and confidante I had been missing in the last few years.

---

1. Loose shirt
2. An Indian sweet made from a mixture of flour, sugar, and shortening, which is shaped into a ball
3. An Indian confectioner
4. Rolling pin
5. The forest where Lord Krishna danced with the gopis
6. Scarf
7. Belonging to the films
8. Where are you from?
9. Your mother and father?
10. They still live there. They threw me out.

11. But why?
12. Because I'm a widow.
13. Tea
14. At least take a look... I've made it myself...
15. Almonds
16. A formal suit originating from the state of Jodhpur
17. Indian flat bread
18. An ornamental wristband given during the Indian festival of Raksha Bandhan as an amulet or token of respect and affection, typically by a woman or girl to her brother or a man that she regards as a brother
19. A flat, thick piece of unleavened bread fried on a griddle
20. Everything will be alright.
21. Kohl

V

There was an invocation to the God of dance, *Nataraj*[1], right at the start. Bindra performed it along with Priya and a few of her favourite students. The Home Minister was seated in the front row with Mrs Padhi and another teacher flanking him. He looked bored. I guessed this was just another routine thing he had to tick off his list of must-do public events. He didn't seem to be the sort of person who was interested in dance-dramas.

Some of the foreign visitors sat behind him, looking far more engaged and impressed. A bit of colour and culture never failed to awe the uninitiated. Did they truly want to understand our mythology and symbolism, or was this just a way for them to briefly experience the exotic, claiming for themselves the labels of the well travelled and refined?

Invocation done, the drama began in earnest. As back-up dancers, we twirled onto the stage. We were the multiple *gopis*[2] sent to fetch water from the banks of the river Yamuna. We danced and chatted amongst ourselves, filling our pretend-pots with pretend-water, till Priya shimmered into view. The most beauteous of the *gopis*, she was playing the part of Radha. She looked forlorn as her beau, the flirtatious *Kanhaiyya*[3] was yet to make an appearance. We teased her about her love, telling her through our dance moves that he was a fickle lover, that he would break her heart one day. Still, she waited, in the vain hope that he would appear.

Scene segued into scene, the backdrops, costumes and dancers changing each time. Every time I was onstage I would peer into the audience, trying to spot Ma and Papa, to no avail. I could not understand it. It was well past 8 p.m. now and nearing the halfway break. They'd always arrived on-time for *didi's* shows and sat up front. Where were they?

During the interval I asked Vandy to go look for them. She gave me a funny look, but setting the bundle of skirts aside, went out obediently. Ten minutes later she came back shaking her head. They were nowhere to be seen. Why weren't they here? Could something have happened? Could they have argued? Maybe Papa didn't come home in time. Yes, that must be it. But they could still have tried to make it, even just to catch a little bit of the show. What about our dinner? No, wait... no one had actually mentioned dinner. I had just assumed we would do what we'd always done. Had that just been wishful thinking on my part?

Thoughts and emotions churned inside of me, but I tried to keep my composure. Someone offered me an apple slice and I chewed on it morosely. Was I not even worth this much: a mere attendance? I suppose I had always been second best, I'd known and accepted that all my life. Why would things be any different now?

THE SECOND HALF OF THE SHOW BEGAN WITH RADHA sitting by the banks of the Yamuna (painted enthusiastically by Mr Bose's year eight students). She was plaiting her hair, still waiting for her elusive lover to show. Forest noises surrounded her, as a plaintive song about unrequited love rang out in the background.

Suddenly, a beautiful peacock appeared. Radha sat still, not wanting to startle it. It strutted around the forest, head raised, almost as though it was listening to a quiet whisper in the leaves. Then it shook out its exquisite tail and quivering with anticipation, began the rain dance.

The girl enacting the part of the peacock was a recent entrant to our school. Still very young, only twelve, she had been plucked out of obscurity by Bindra on the basis of a single dance rehearsal. I'll never forget the way our mouths had fallen open when we'd first seen her perform the rain dance; her effortless grace, the fluidity of her movements, her ability to transfix her audience. With a stage presence Priya could only hope to emulate, this dance was easily the highlight of the show, and each time we watched her perform it, we were riveted.

I looked out at the audience from the wings and could sense the wonderment that had descended upon them. It was not dissimilar to what we were feeling, despite having seen her performance many times in rehearsals.

Radha faded into the background as the peacock spun and whirled on the stage, its tail fanning out behind it, plumes fully spread, the spotlight fixed firmly upon it.

THE RAIN DANCE WAS ABOUT HOPE, EXPECTANCY AND JOY. The peacock could sense the advent of the monsoon and declared it to one and all through its restless dance. In the midst of the dance, the sound of Krishna's melodious flute emerged unexpectedly from the painted thicket, sending the peacock into a frenzy. It twirled round and round wildly till stopping in front of the Lord as he stood there, flute in hand, making his first appearance upon the stage. For just a moment, there was complete silence. Then the peacock bowed its head in the presence of divinity, offering up a feather as its token of love and devotion. *Kanhaiyya* accepted it gracefully, placing it upon his *mukut*[4], thus completing the picture of the mythological Krishna us Indians worship.

As the peacock left the stage, the spotlight moved to Sunil, who stood there in his Krishna pose, flute in hand, legs crossed at the ankles, peacock feather in his crown. A common sigh reverberated in the audience. Here at last was the elusive Lord!

What went through Sunil's mind at that moment? Did he have a single moment of reservation about what he was about to do? A moment perhaps where sabotage receded and a desire to please tried to overtake him? We would never know. For, from that sublime moment, the dance-drama descended into the most ridiculous farce anyone could have envisaged.

It started with Radha approaching Krishna, awe and wonder writ large in her movements. This was the epicentre of her universe, her beloved, her everything, and in her pining she encompassed all of humanity's longing to be one with the Divine. Priya's steps were graceful; her movements as light as a butterfly's wings. Sunil was meant to stand still in his pose while she circled him, conveying her reverence. Instead, he started to sway on the spot, losing his balance and slamming into her. For a moment, Priya stumbled. Then, regaining her balance, she threw him a confused look and began the next dance.

This was the dance of Radha and Krishna's romance, immortalised in text, music and legend. This was also Bindra's labour of love: something they had slaved over in rehearsal after rehearsal, that which had transformed Sunil's two left feet into some imitation of a dancer, also what had created the rift between Sunil and Jasmin, and what Bindra had hoped would be the pièce de résistance of the entire show.

For every one of Radha's graceful moves, Krishna's seemed utterly discombobulated. If she approached, he retreated, if she stood still, he gyrated. The dance grew increasingly bizarre, bearing no recognition to the one that had been practised to present to the crowd.

Priya tried her best to salvage it, this much I'd give her credit for. Yet, there was no distracting Sunil from his purpose. Here was Krishna in another *avatar*[5]! Missing each of his cues, Sunil incorporated various dance forms into the choreography. He jived, he mamboed, he swayed like a man on drugs. This was Krishna on a high, and poor Radha had nary a clue what to do with him.

All of us watched the dance disintegrate in shock and horror. I didn't want to imagine what would happen to Sunil afterwards, but a part of me couldn't help but applaud his courage. It was no mean feat to show Bindra up in front of so many people.

I glanced over to where she stood. Her face was like thunder. After the initial shock, she must have realised what Sunil was up to, but it was too late to do anything about it, without ruining the entire choreography. So, she let it carry on, but her posture had stiffened, and I knew there would be a reckoning.

I peered at the audience to see how this performance was going down. People looked bemused. They whispered amongst themselves, some of them were laughing, others pointing and nodding, someone even whistled. As Sunil's movements got even more rock-and-roll-like, Priya finally had enough and walked off the stage in tears. One of the teachers, trying her best, ushered all of us out instead. "Go dance", she urged.

So, a flock of us *gopis* perambulated onto the stage. Since none of us knew quite what to do, each of us improvised and did whatever came to our minds.

I shuffled over to Sunil and whispered, "What the heck are you doing?"

"Exacting revenge." He winked at me and clambered on to the side stage, holding on to a painted branch of a tree that made the entire back set sway precariously.

Just before the whole set crashed to the floor, someone turned the lights off. There was pin-drop silence and then the hooting and cheering started up in the audience. In the darkness, we scrambled to pull the set upright under Mr Bose's whispered instructions. I could hear hushed weeping amongst the girls. Some of them had put their hearts and souls into their performances, only to see it descend into chaos like this. I felt like slapping Sunil. I understood his reasons, but could not justify his actions.

We trailed off the stage and then the lights were turned back on. The set looked slightly askew, but not too bad considering the circumstances. Sunil was nowhere to be seen. Mrs Padhi, our Principal, had gone totally pale. This was the point where she should have walked up to the stage to thank the dancers and introduce the minister. But she sat still on her chair, rooted to the spot. After a brief spell, the Home Minister stood up of his own volition and walked to the stage. Someone hastily brought out a microphone for him to speak into.

"Well, I can honestly say, I have never enjoyed a performance better!" He grinned as he looked at the audience. "When I was invited here this evening, I thought I'd have to sit through another predictable dance-drama, but how much fun was this?! I had no idea this was going to be a comedy. That Krishna... where is he? I'd like to give him a pat on his back! Our Lord was always known to be *natkhat*[6], but today, I truly saw that in action."

"Well done, all of you! This was unexpected but I am so impressed. Thank you and good night." The audience started cheering and clapping, and as his retinue led him out, he turned and waved to all of us in the wings, a knowing gleam in his eyes.

As we packed up, I could see Mrs Padhi and Bindra in heated conversation by the side of the stage. I couldn't see Sunil anywhere. He must have escaped at some point, but Monday was only three days away, and there would be Hell to pay three days from now. Jasmin sidled up to me, her face red from laughing.

"Did you know he was going to do that?" I asked her.

"I had an inkling that he was going to mess it up somehow, but not to the extent he did. What a nutcase!" She was still full of mirth but sobered up at the expression on my face. "I mean, he did take it too far..."

"You can say that again!" I was angry, but not sure who the anger was directed towards – my two idiotic friends or my missing parents.

Vandy had gone out looking for them again and hadn't returned yet. If they weren't here how were we to get home?

A year eight student approached us. "Are you Puja Sharma?"

"Yes."

"Two people are asking for you outside."

My heartbeat quickened. Maybe Vandy had missed them and they'd been there all along. I picked up my stuff and mouthed a quick goodbye to Jasmin, rushing out to ask my parents what they'd thought of our shambolic show.

I ground to a halt as my little messenger pointed to the couple standing by the side of the stage. Vandy stood by them, looking just as perplexed as I was feeling. Sujata aunty and Onir had come to fetch us. Sujata aunty and Onir? What on Earth, and why??

. . .

THE TAXI THEY'D HIRED WAS WAITING IN THE CAR PARK, the meter still running. Onir sat up front as Vandy and I slid in on either side of Sujata aunty.

"What's going on? Why are you two here?"

"Yes, Mumma, why are you here? You and Papa weren't coming? I was supposed to take a ride with Puja and her family?" Vandy chimed in at the exact same moment.

"Something's happened," Sujata aunty threw a look at the taxi driver as she whispered this to us. "I can't talk about it right now."

"Are my parents okay?"

"Yes, they are fine Puja. They sent us to collect you."

"But why didn't they come themselves?"

Onir turned around. "Because something has happened! Can't you girls just wait a while before we explain everything?"

I glared at his back. Why the Hell was he here anyway? Mr High-and-Mighty Author, whose one published book languished unsold on bookstore shelves. Who was he to preach patience to us?

What could have happened? It must be serious or they would have told us by now. Vandy and I exchanged a quick glance, but Sujata aunty sat Sphinx-like between us and we didn't get a chance to voice our frustration.

The taxi rattled on, all its occupants silent, except for the driver who spat out the excess spittle from the *paan*[7] in his mouth out of his window in a rather dramatic fashion. I watched the streak of orange spittle fly by me and shuddered in disgust. Why was this journey taking forever?

WHEN WE PULLED UP IN FRONT OF THE HOUSE, ALL THE lights were on. There were people going in and out of our doorway, and the locality stray dogs kept barking at the hubbub. I ran out of the taxi, barely waiting for Onir to stop haggling with the driver over the fare. Vandy and Sujata aunty followed hurriedly.

I pushed past the neighbours crowding the hallway, towards Papa, who was sitting in his armchair with his head in his hands. Vandy's father and another man stood next to him, talking in undertones.

"W... what's happened?"

He looked up at me, his face stricken. "Puja..."

Sujata aunty steered me away from him, towards my bedroom.

"Let me explain, Puja."

"No! Where's Ma? What's going on? Why is everyone here?"

I heard Krishna crying and instinctively ran towards Ma's room.

She sat on her bed rocking him in her arms, tears spilling from her eyes as the women milled around her, offering her water, patting her back, whispering in her ears. I looked at the scene in confusion. Had I wandered into some sort of twilight zone? Everything seemed familiar, yet not really.

"Ma...?"

She looked up at me and her face seemed to crumple. A low moan escaped her and ever so gently, she keeled over to one side and fainted. One of the ladies grabbed Krishna from her lap, while another lifted her feet onto the bed.

Sujata aunty put her arm around my shoulder and led me to my room once again. She handed me a cup of hot, sweet tea. My teeth started to chatter suddenly, the ominous feeling I'd harboured all day threatening to overtake me.

"Puja, sit down please. Let me explain."

Her voice seemed to be coming from far, far away. It felt like I was in a tunnel, being sucked backwards, the air whooshing past me, darkness pressing down upon me. Everything seemed surreal: the colour of my curtains too red, the sheet under my hands too rough, the light in the lamp too bright, the voices outside weirdly cacophonous and my heartbeat, loud and insistent, drowning out her words, submerging this grotesque reality under layers and layers of shock, disbelief and disorientation.

LOYALTY WAS ALL LAKSHMI HAD EVER HAD TO OFFER. WAS it loyalty that had led her to the Mehtas' house? Was it loyalty or justice that had made her confront them with the truth of Krishna's paternity? Surely Lakshmi had not had the ability to lie or dissemble. But why expose herself in this manner? Why confront the perpetrator in his own lair?

"She could not take your mother's distress. She must have felt the need to do something."

"Was she lying, or is Mr Mehta truly Krishna's father?"

"We don't know, and I guess now we'll never know for sure. But Mrs Mehta accused her of being a *naali ki kutti*[8], a *randi*[9] and a whole host of horrible things. It got very, very ugly."

"How do you know all of this, Sujata aunty?"

"Onir has told us everything. He was there and he saw it all."

It was past midnight and everyone had left. Ma had managed to calm a fractious Krishna with a hastily bought and assembled bottle of milk. He lay asleep on the bed, his little fist curled around Ma's finger. Papa, Sujata aunty, Vandy, Vandy's dad, Onir and I were the only ones left trying to make sense of it all.

"What were you doing at the Mehtas?" Papa asked Onir, a weary suspicion tinging his question.

Onir looked down shamefacedly.

"I was helping him with the advertisement he wanted placed in the newspaper."

"To do with the election?"

"No. To do with you."

"Ah! So the rumours were true."

"Yes, I'm sorry, I needed the money."

"And you had no qualms about vilifying my dead daughter or our family?"

Onir stayed silent.

"What did Lakshmi say?" I spat the words out, not bothering to hide my disgust.

"The maid must have let her in because suddenly she was there, in the room where we'd been discussing the ad. She placed the baby at Mr Mehta's feet and said '*aapka bachcha*[10].'" Onir spoke softly. "Mrs Mehta went mad with fury. She started screaming at them both, saying she had always suspected something was amiss. Saying that it was Mr Mehta who had insisted on hiring and relocating Lakshmi. She started hitting Lakshmi while Mr Mehta sat like a statue, the baby wailing at his feet. Lakshmi took the beating submissively till Mrs Mehta kicked the baby. At that point she snatched him up and tried leaving."

"What happened then?" Ma choked the words out, although she already knew.

"Mrs Mehta tried grabbing the baby out of Lakshmi's arms saying how she'd dash his head to the floor and kill him. She was hysterical and threatening to kill everyone in the room! I think Lakshmi got scared. I mean, I was scared... the woman was behaving like a maniac..."

He paused, as though to collect his thoughts.

"Lakshmi ran out of the house, with the baby in her arms. Mrs Mehta ran behind her. I gave chase to them as I wasn't sure what she was going to do to that poor woman and her baby. They had a tussle on the street, and people started to come out of their houses to see what the fracas was about. I tried separating them, but it was futile and honestly, I couldn't make out who was hitting, who was scratching and who was screaming!"

There was a tremor in his voice as he continued.

"Lakshmi must've gotten loose at some point because she tore away on to the street without looking either side."

"That's when the car hit her." Sujata aunty pronounced this slowly. "She must have turned her body just in time to save Krishna, but she took the full impact."

"She died on the spot. I picked the baby up, and held him until the police arrived." Onir looked close to tears.

"And the Mehtas?" I asked, almost as an afterthought.

"Mr Mehta never came outside at all. Mrs Mehta saw the accident, but then went back inside and locked the door. They haven't come out since."

"Lakshmi was taken to the hospital but pronounced dead on arrival. The police came to talk to us, but what could we tell them?" Papa looked exhausted as he said this. "Now, we just have this poor motherless baby who will probably have to go to an orphanage."

I looked at Krishna, sleeping peacefully on my parents' bed, and wept softly at the unfairness of it all.

LIFE IS LIKE A LOTTERY WITH RANDOM NUMBERS ASSIGNED to each of us. Some are fortunate enough to be winners, to have it all – love, luck, felicity and prosperity. And others live and die in misery, grasping at the corners of happiness, never quite being able to hold on or to claim it as their own. Who assigns these numbers to us and why? Is it a benevolent God or a vindictive one? Is it our own *karma*[11] or just some strange universal logic that we cannot comprehend?

What would become of this innocent baby who had only

known his mother's love for a few weeks? I closed my eyes. There were no more tears to shed nor any prayers to give. Hopelessness washed over me, and I felt bone-weary at the futility of everything. Why, oh why, did we do anything at all, if all we were really doing was hurtling towards our own demise? What was the point of any of it?

I observed the people around me; at my parents who looked older than their years, at Sujata aunty who sat next to my mother, talking softly, repeatedly patting her hand, at Onir who lurked near the door, wanting to escape but unable to leave, at Vandy and her dad, exhausted but still here, still supporting us, and then my glance fell upon Krishna once again. For a brief time Lakshmi and Krishna had brought joy and promise into our lives. There had been a new life to focus on, and momentarily we had put our own woes behind us and welcomed them into our fold. Had Lakshmi's love and sacrifice been totally in vain?

Papa ushered Onir out and Ma hugged Sujata aunty as she left with her family, and suddenly, unexpectedly, in the midst of all the sadness and despair, somewhere within me a little spark of hope ignited itself. Nothing good was ever truly lost. Just as we would always carry *didi* within us, we would also carry the memories of the brief time Lakshmi spent with us. In some shape or form, Krishna would know his mother and what she did for him. And us.

I lay down next to him, watching his little chest rise and fall, my mind and body numb with fatigue, but with a strange, strong resolve growing inside of me. Breathing in his sweet baby smell, I allowed myself to be lulled into sleep alongside.

2019

"HONESTLY PUJA, CAN YOU JUST COME OVER FOR A second?"

"Ingrid, you are better at this stuff. I really don't care one way or another…"

In the silence that followed, I knew I was being judged and found wanting.

"Okay," I sighed with resignation, dropping my research paper to the floor and coming towards the laptop.

I could only see the top of Ma's head, with her wiry grey hair springing up in all directions.

"Ma, I can't see you! Lower the screen."

Her face swam into view as she frowned at me. "All I'm asking you to do is pick the colour. I'll get everything else done."

"Fine! Just show me the *saris*. I mean, really! Who cares what I'll be wearing? Surely it's about Krish and Rohini? They are the ones getting married!"

"But you are coming to India after two years, and you are his elder sister. Of course, everyone will be looking at you too."

"Ma, they'll be looking at me for other reasons, and you know that."

"Puja, nobody cares! India has moved forward. We have many Lebanese people here too." She said this proudly albeit a bit defensively.

I looked at Ingrid and sighed. She giggled. She thought it was funny.

"Ma, for the nth time! It's Lesbian, not Lebanese. Besides, we'd much rather be called gay."

"Well, as long as you are happy. Although I don't know what Papa would have made of it. Krish keeps telling me that Papa would have been fine… God bless his departed soul."

"Where is Krish anyway?"

"Yes, yes, one minute…"

A familiar dark face popped up on the screen.

"*Didi*! How are you?"

"I'm fine, but how's my baby brother doing? Not driving his bride-to-be crazy with his demands, I hope?"

"As if! Ro is the bridezilla... she's micromanaging the lot. But she and Ma have it all under control and Vandy *didi* has been helping loads. Can't wait to see you and Ingrid soon! Did you know that Sunil and Jas are coming for the wedding too, along with the twins?"

"Yes, they rang me a few days ago. It'll be good to catch up with them. We'll be there in two weeks bro, and please, no garlands and *tikkas*[12] at the airport this time!"

"Haha! Okay. Love you *didi*. Speak soon."

He signed off, his mismatched eyes twinkling with glee.

Ingrid came up behind me and nuzzled my neck.

"Ready for dinner?"

I turned and smiled.

"Yes love, ready."

---

1. The God of dance
2. Female cowherds, lovers of Krishna with whom he dances at the time of the autumn moon
3. Another name for Krishna
4. Crown/Diadem
5. Incarnation
6. Mischievous
7. Betel leaves
8. A bitch from the gutters
9. Whore
10. Your child
11. (in Hinduism and Buddhism) The sum of a person's actions in this and previous states of existence, viewed as deciding their fate in future existences
12. A mark on the forehead made with with sandal paste or kumkum

AFTERWORD

Word-of-mouth is crucial for any author to succeed. If you enjoyed the book, please do leave a review on Amazon and Goodreads. Even if it's just a star rating or a sentence or two, it would make all the difference and would be very much appreciated.

www.goodreads.com

www.amazon.com

www.amazon.uk

www.amazon.in

This novella started its life as a short story. A story that set up residence in my mind, when a few years ago I had woken up one morning wondering, whatever happened to that sweeper woman? Yes, a long time ago, there had been a sweeper woman and her little boy who had inhabited our locality for a very brief time. No one knew where they came from or where they eventually went and I was much too young to ask questions.

However, something about her plight must have lodged in my mind, for nearly forty years later, I got to expand upon her story in my way.

The many injustices that I explore or briefly alight upon are not restricted to the era of this tale. They have occurred throughout history, whether in the East or the West. They continue to occur. Women being ill-treated, marginalised or vilified happens at every stratum of society. The irony is, that without women there would be no society.

What we must do is confront the status quo and in some small way try to alleviate the suffering of our sisterhood. How can that happen? By building bridges of understanding and compassion and by reaching out in love and kindness to those less fortunate than us.

So, while there is much loss in this book, there is also a lot of love and hope. Isn't that what all life is comprised of?

ACKNOWLEDGMENTS

This book is what it is thanks to my wonderful editor, Charulatha Dasappa. Through the many sessions of editing, re-editing, WhatsApp chats and Skype calls, she polished my first draft into this novella. She made me re-examine my ideas, reinforce the weaker parts and structure the tale suitably. All the while, being very patient with my varying schedules and missed deadlines. Charu, you are truly a gem!

The cover art is by Team Miblart who transformed my vision for the cover into the beautiful design you see today.

A shout out to the many Indie writers groups on Facebook, who help and encourage other Indies, and assisted me in finding my editor, my cover art team and weighed in on my burb. A fabulous network that I am so lucky to be a part of.

Finally, nothing would be possible without the love and support of my family and friends. Thank you!

If you would like to contact Charulatha or Team Miblart, their details are as follows:

charu.dpp@gmail.com
team@miblart.com

ABOUT THE AUTHOR

Always a voracious reader, Poornima started writing at the age of eight and never really stopped, although there were many dry spells.

She found her writing voice in 2009 when a short story of hers placed in an online competition run by The Guardian newspaper. Having re-discovered her first love, she started her online blog at www.poornimamanco.wordpress.com.

Initially, she published many of her stories, thoughts and musings there. In 2018, she decided to take a leap of faith into Indie publishing and compiled her stories into two separate books as a part of a trilogy. She is currently at work on the third book of short stories.

Most of her tales are set in India as her formative years were spent there. Born and brought up in New Delhi, she moved to the United Kingdom in her twenties. Yet, she has never been able to cut the umbilical cord that ties her to her birthplace.

She loves reading, travelling and the company of good friends. She is married and has two teenage daughters.

Parvathy's Well & other stories

Damage

REVIEWS OF PARVATHY'S WELL & OTHER STORIES:

- What can I say about this deliciously beautiful book? Its a real gem, beautifully written, colourful, taking me back to India. Could feel it all around me, through the surprising and dramatic twists of the stories. Nothing is as it seems, never knew where the stories would lead. Very much looking forward to more of Poornima's work!

- What a great read! Didn't want to put it down once I started reading it. Takes you on a journey to India giving you a snippet of the different layers of Indian society and its norms, each story telling a tale set in a different setting of the Indian society. Myriad of emotions reading the short stories – poignant and nostalgic while also feeling pained and saddened with some aspects of the human psyche and behaviour, that have been depicted so realistically through the characters in the stories.

- Poornima's stories are an evocative kaleidoscope of life in India touching upon various social issues. They are haunting , soul searching and brutally honest tales of human weaknesses and strength . There is an honesty to the characters that does not shy away from laying bare their vulnerabilities or moral fabric. Her style is engaging and free flowing with a fluidity that makes her stories very pleasurable to read. I am eagerly looking forward to the next instalment !

- Some stories were disturbing and some insightful but they were all engrossing. I liked that they were easy to read because of the spacing and length. Waiting to read more by this author.

- Parvathy's well, Manco's maiden publication takes the reader on an emotional journey into the lives of the protagonists and their daily trials and tribulations. Each of the characters and situations seem very real and believable indicating author's grasp of the subject and familiarity with the Indian sub-continental culture that the stories are set in. The high quality of Manco's writing belies this being only her debut book and I hope she follows it up with further works and deservedly be recognised as an accomplished writer in the literary circles soon.

- Poornima's short stories bring a kaleidoscope of colors, smells and characters that are uniquely Indian. The short stories are poignant and complex, shining a light on the darkness behind the mundane everyday lives of ordinary people . Each story captures and enthrals the imagination. Can't wait to read many more stories from the author!

- A very well written book. It's gripping, in someplaces dark but has you absorbed from page one till the very end. It brings to life the India I grew up in, with all her complexities, traditions.Poornima has a unique ability to bring the characters to life and lend them complex layers. I'm looking forward to Ms. Mancos' next book. Wishing her all the very best in her next venture.

- A glorious set of six short stories! Such beautifully written tales. They will lure you in and lull you with the language, only to surprise and startle you when you least expect it. Each story will leave you wanting more and I cannot wait for the next book!

- Poornima's stories are so full of life and description that I felt I experienced a bit of the Indian culture and country I have longed to visit for many years. That voyage is now at the top of my list.Her writing is so insightful that although the character's names and places where the stories took place were all set in India, the events, feelings, and lessons were quite ubiquitous. Even if India is a country and culture much removed from your own, it is easy to relate to and become one with the characters as they go on their journey.There is nothing better than when a story or book causes you to analyze, challenge, and decide for yourself what the ending and the lesson learned is. This book has that in spades. I am waiting with much anticipation for more from Poornima!

- Finished Parvathy's Well and other stories. Also read the printed reviews and I can genuinely say I totally agree, Poornima Manco grabs the reader and takes them on an engrossing journey from the very first paragraph. We her subjects hang on to every beautifully written word, transported to a world inhabited by instantly compelling humans. Yes, humans, love them or hate them they are to multi dimensional to be merely characters. That is an astonishing feat given the short length of any one of the stories. Her compelling writing is exactly why I have a problem, her ability to engage our emotions is painful when we are left full of sorrow and impotence. There was so much of it! totally unresolved, left screaming on the pages, hanging in there like an accusation to our cruel and fallible common humanity. It is a personal quirk of mine that I will tolerate any amount of pain as long as redemption is interspersed with it, I know that my need for a happy ending is unrealistic and totally infantile. I just can't help it, Poornima Manco's writing made my heart hurt. In that I believe that the purpose of good writing is to engage our emotions, she has totally succeeded,

REVIEWS FOR DAMAGE:

- Poornima Manco's second collection of short stories under the title Damage (India Book 2) will leave you somewhat damaged emotionally. Most of the stories revealing heartbreaking events which again are all set in India. Just when you think it can't get any worse it does. Wishing the stories to be entirely fiction, having a close connection with India myself, I know they are sadly based on true events. Each story has a hidden message which leaves the reader wondering how life can be so cruel yet so soul searching at same time. As with Manco's first collection I'm left with a desire for more as she draws you into each chapter furiously yet abandons you just as quickly, leaving you with a myriad of unanswered questions...

- Another beautifully written book by this author. The content is often dark but the humanity of the characters and the occasional humour lift these tales away from being only tragic. Each story will affect you in a different way from the dreaminess of 'Ma Vie Sans Couleur' to the stark horror of 'Swami Claus' and the creepiness of 'Creep'! Eagerly awaiting the third installment...

- Definitely not for the faint hearted! Brutally honest and compelling. Revealing and truthful, this book will spook you out and have you hooked until its very last word. One can never be too sure of the outcome of a story from this author; she is truly the master of plot twists!

- Most stories had me stunned. They seemed to be about people I almost knew so left me sad about how their lives evolved, how they used others or got used by many and those who barely found happiness. Why are humans so ruthless to each other when we know that we're all made the same way, with skin, bones, emotions and in this world only for a certain period?

- Poornima Manco's Damage is a book where the characters are driven to their destinies through themes of rejection, isolation, ignorance, violence and poverty to create stories that will reverberate in your mind to the spine chilling conclusion of Swami Claus, the sadness of Ugly to the utter heart breaking devastation of Like a Boss. This author is someone who creates a world that we sometimes recognise and although fiction, says it just,"as it

Is", and although sometimes shocking and dark her writing is always REAL.

- A very poignant and dark journey into the lives of damaged people and how their cultural making can drive them to explore and even experience their darkest inner self in a plethora of short stories set in India. The author successfully embarks us in this whirlwind of darkness by depicting real emotions in her characters which makes us love them, hate them or feel for them, but you will be touched, you will feel sadness, and even disgust at times, but you will for sure close this book and have felt something deep. Can't wait for the next book!!

- A collection of compelling short stories about the darkness that seems to hide behind the facade of ordinary lives. Poornima builds the stories delicately layering them with details that transport me to the streets of India. The characters are ordinary and yet their lives take sometimes macabre turns and at other times just sad paths. Poornima does not try to shock or trick us. Her stories have a realism and though sometimes disturbing they always ring true.

- The book is wonderful and transports me to the heat, dust and (sometimes) squalor of rural India. I am almost tempted to start swatting flies as I turn the pages! The stories portray the dark side of Indian culture ie. child abuse, wife beating, and misogyny, which I find deeply sad and disturbing in my warm, happy, content life in middle England. I yearn for a happy ending!

- This lady is a brilliant writer. True to life stories reflecting the real & unpredictable world we live in. Not for the faint hearted, no where to hide, she has touched on politics both inside & outside of family life in India. Having read her first book 'Parvathy's Well & other stories this was also pure brilliance. Bracing myself for her next book...if I dare!!!!!

- Dark, compelling stories which transport us to India. The author's writing has matured and her stories are chilling but uncomfortably realistic. Universal themes of human depravity and fragility mixed with Indian culture, fascinating and disturbing. I cannot wait for the next book.

- The second book of short stories from Poornima does not disappoint! It takes you to India through the smells, sounds, colours, can feel the air! The stories are full of dark turns and twists, never knowing where it will all lead, but always surprised how it turned out. I really didn't want it to end, the stories drew me in, taking me there. A real gem of a book!!

- DAMAGE, by Poornima Manco, is a well and sensitively written collection of 16 short stories about individuals trying to exist in modern culture while largely unable to escape the their traditional Indian one. These are characters you know, but do you really know them? They now inhabit a world including extended international family and dominated by easy travel, instant communication and social media. Sadly, however, technology doesn't change the rules but merely makes them easier to break. Despite the variety of settings, the characters are all weary and restless. They must live by rules that are no longer relevant and are fighting against meaningless conformity.

Deception, particularly self deception, deludes characters overwhelmed by powerful often violent emotions and the results of their obsessions and subsequent choices are often tragic. Occasionally, because of these traditions and rules, they still assume guilt for the results of ensuing events not really their fault such as in Damage, the first story for which the collection is named. At the heart of nearly every story is a man (on the basis of his sex only) privileged with far more power and choices than the women around him. Each one is selfish and pursues a voracious appetite be he the son of an abandoned grandmother in 'The Strings That Bind Us', the exploitative swami in 'Swami Claus', the narcissistic lothario in 'Unlikely Casanova', Amar, the murdering mad brother, in 'Jehadi Love', Rahul, who chooses the daughter over the mother, in 'The Consequence of Contradiction', or the depraved letch in 'Creep', etc. Interestingly, they all find a woman or women to blame for their selfish and heartless actions whether it be a lover, mother, sister, daughter or wife. Only Damu in 'Secrets and Lies' seems to able escape this masculine curse but not without being saddled with the responsibility of everyone else's sadness and losses by his god playing putative father. The women depicted in the stories are mostly less powerful and thus subject to the twists and turns of fate, their behavior often contradictory in their voracious craving for love and subsequent regretful relationships. They surge with turbulent emotions but are frequently betrayed and sometimes by themselves. They stand the most to gain in future by freeing themselves from the system but also the most to lose in the present. Love and sex are powerful seductive drugs, but a bad reputation can ruin them forever. This submerges them in worlds of complicated, sometimes impenetrable fantasy and fabrication. The more intimate the relationships, the greater the deceptions. One story that stands out in the collection is Palindrome. Nayan has achieved independence, power and success but still happiness and love elude her. She is painfully self aware but even self realisation cannot save her. Doomed, she, too, sadly loses hope in the human condition and her ability to change it. The stories in Damage collectively pose the question: are all of us damaged in some way, and if so are we damaged solely because of our personal choices or because of our inability to escape the entrenched representations of traditional culture, class, family, religion, politics and sex? Every so often a laser beam of absolute clarity reveals an answer from within the layers of compounded entangled emotions of humanity's dark side depicted in these stories.

- Years ago, when I first read 'Memoirs of a Geisha', I felt like I had been taken on a journey to Japan. Poornima Manco's novels give me that exact same feeling about India: it is as if you are there, completely immersed in its climate and culture. 'Damage', the author's second book of the India trilogy, consists of 16 short stories. They are all very different - some long, some short - which is what makes the book so interesting and unpredictable. However, there are some common themes: of unhappy marriages; of secrets, pleasure and guilt; of children letting down parents and vice versa; of women of a certain age, and whether or not they've still 'got it'; of entitled and misogynistic men; and of hypocrisy and double standards in Indian society. 'Damage' is, just like its predecessor 'Parvathy's Well & Other Stories', very dark. But in a way, that is also its strength, as it allows the author to explore the underbelly of Indian culture. Some of the stories, such as 'Like a Boss', are based on real events that you may have read about in the newspaper. This can make for some uncomfortable reading, as you suddenly recognise the story and know that there is going to be a tragic ending. The main characters in the book are often very complex and not particularly likeable, but they pull you in nevertheless. Take Lolita, the victim of paedophilia in the chilling and brilliantly written 'Swami Claus'. Should we feel sorry for her, because of the damage that was done to her as a child? Or should we simply hate the monster that she has become? Is it wrong that we are pleased that "karma has ridden in on her chariot", and she gets her comeuppance in the end? The power of the story lies in the fact that we feel all of those emotions, which is a testament to the skills of the author. Poornima's writing really seems to be evolving, and I felt that the descriptions of people and situations were spot on. I absolutely love the way she uses the English language, which can paint a picture in just a few sentences. Read, for instance, the first paragraph of 'Creep': "He sidled up to her, crab like in his approach. His shirt was stretched tight over his pot belly, buttons threatening to detonate any moment. 'Hello', he smiled greasily." You don't need to hear anything else, you know straightaway what kind of guy this is. The original and unexpected angles in the book (both a husband and a wife's account of what is essentially a wedding night rape in 'Ugly', for instance), the variety of stories and the author's insight into the human condition meant that I read 'Damage' in one go. I absolutely loved it, and I would definitely recommend it and give it five stars.

Printed in Poland
by Amazon Fulfillment
Poland Sp. z o.o., Wrocław

49132561R00066